OPEN HOUSE

Jean Blue

A Novel

OPEN HOUSE

Open Heart, Open House

© 2007 by Jean Blue. All rights reserved.

Pleasant Word (a division of WinePress Publishing, PO Box 428, Enumclaw, WA 98022) functions only as book publisher. As such, the ultimate design, content, editorial accuracy, and views expressed or implied in this work are those of the author.

No part of this publication may be reproduced, stored in a retrieval system or transmitted in any way by any means—electronic, mechanical, photocopy, recording or otherwise—without the prior permission of the copyright holder, except as provided by USA copyright law.

Unless otherwise noted, all Scriptures are taken from the Holy Bible, New International Version, Copyright © 1973, 1978, 1984 by the International Bible Society. Used by permission of Zondervan Publishing House. The "NIV" and "New International Version" trademarks are registered in the United States Patent and Trademark Office by International Bible Society.

Scripture references marked KJV are taken from the King James Version of the Bible.

Scripture references marked NASB are taken from the New American Standard Bible, © 1960, 1963, 1968, 1971, 1972, 1973, 1975, 1977 by The Lockman Foundation. Used by permission.

ISBN 13: 978-1-4141-0811-7
ISBN 10: 1-4141-0811-7
Library of Congress Catalog Card Number: 2006907072

Dedication

To the many friends in my home church of Faith United Methodist in Barryton, and to all those in the family of God whose friendship has been a blessing.

Table of Contents

Acknowledgements ix

Chapter One: Regrets 11
Chapter Two: On Her Own 25
Chapter Three: The Commitment 33
Chapter Four: House Guest 39
Chapter Five: The Letters 45
Chapter Six: The Search 55
Chapter Seven: Meeting with the Sheriff 61
Chapter Eight: David in Love 65
Chapter Nine: Man in the House 69
Chapter Ten: Conversations 77
Chapter Eleven: Warnings 81
Chapter Twelve: Growing Commitment 87
Chapter Thirteen: The Suspect 91
Chapter Fourteen: The Greatest Gift 95
Chapter Fifteen: The Past Uncovered 101
Chapter Sixteen: The Twins 107
Chapter Seventeen: Fear and Faith 113
Chapter Eighteen: Luncheon Discussion 119
Chapter Nineteen: Phone Call 125

Chapter Twenty: Evening to Remember 129
Chapter Twenty One: The Love of Cars 135
Chapter Twenty Two: Lost and Found 143
Chapter Twenty Three: Good News 151
Chapter Twenty Four: Thanksgiving Revelations 157
Chapter Twenty Five: Mom and That Man Kelley 167
Chapter Twenty Six: Tom and David 175

Epilogue 179

ACKNOWLEDGEMENTS

My thanks to all those at the Winepress Publishing Group, especially Susan K. Marlow, for her editing, and Joseph Ellis for his patience.

Chapter One

REGRETS

The phone rang, and Liz heaved a sigh of relief. She welcomed a reprieve from the silence that seemed to hang from the ceilings, threatening to smother her. What did it matter that she was up to her elbows in bread dough? Brassy, lying at her feet, lifted his shaggy head and then flopped it back down on her feet. She guessed it was Cory calling. Who else would call her at eight in the morning?

"Hey, Girl, whatcha up to?" Her guess was right. Cory's bell-like voice was unmistakable.

"Talking to you. And kneading bread."

"You have a freezer full already."

"I'm getting prepared for Thanksgiving and Christmas. David and Jessie will be coming home from college, you know. They love it. What's up with you?"

"Same old, same old. I was hoping you might be open to some early Christmas shopping."

"Have you looked outside? The ground is covered with snow." Liz eased her feet from beneath Brassy's head and turned to check weather conditions outside the bay window over the sink. Snowflakes swirled around until they landed, carpeting the yard. The pine boughs were beginning to hang under the burden of white fluff. To humor her, Damon had left several pines standing when they built the house. White pines were her favorite trees.

Cory ignored her weather report like so much wet laundry left out to dry. "There must be something going on in town. I hear sirens. I'm sure you can't hear them out there in the woods." Cory hadn't a mean bone in her body, but her words hit a nerve.

"No. I don't hear a thing. As always. Like dullsville." The only sounds she heard were the faint whirring of the refrigerator and Brassy's snoring. "I'm glad you called. I've been dying to tell you what happened yesterday when I was grocery shopping."

"What could possibly happen at the grocery store? Were they giving away groceries?"

"No, silly! I was accosted by this dreadful woman."

"You're kidding! What did she do? Steal your groceries?"

"No. I wish I were kidding. I was in the produce department when this woman parked her cart in front of mine. I couldn't get around her. She asked me how I dared go out in public. I was so shocked I just stood there. I'm sure my face was red as a beet. I was so embarrassed."

"I can imagine," Cory agreed.

It was nice having a friend who always took your side. "I said I didn't have any idea what she was talking about. She said I *did* know what she was talking about. Then she sneered at me, 'Don't try to look innocent!'"

"I said I was sorry, that I didn't have the faintest idea what she was talking about. She started yelling, 'Give me a break. You know your employees will be out of work and looking for jobs when *you* close the plant. And what will *you* and your husband be doing? Living high like you do now. Without any worries.'"

"She must be a sick one. Accosting you in public like that," Cory sympathized.

"I told her that my husband handles the business and I had nothing to do with closing the plant, but she wouldn't believe me. Other shoppers were staring at us. It was embarrassing. I asked her to move her cart. She refused. There was no reasoning with her, but I thought I had to try. I told her I hoped her husband found work soon. She exploded, raved like a wild woman, said my kind makes her sick, and said to tell my husband he's the lowest of the low."

"Sounds like she needs an attitude adjustment," Cory gave her opinion.

"You won't believe what I said then. I'm ashamed of myself."

"Knowing you, I'm sure it can't be that bad."

"I told her to move her cart, or I'd ram her."

"Well, good for you!" Cory crowed with delight.

"What was even worse, some shoppers applauded. I'm not proud of myself. What if she showed up in church? I didn't behave any better than she did. She did move her cart then—to my relief. I didn't have everything on my list, but I hurried and checked out."

"She sounds like a lost soul. All we can do is pray for her."

"I suppose," Liz agreed. "And thanks for listening." She was switching the phone to a shoulder and ear position when she saw the sheriff's car rolling up her gravel drive. "The sheriff is coming! I wonder what he's coming here for? I hope nothing has happened to one of my kids." She began imagining the worst possible scenario.

"To your house?"

"We're the only house around here." She hadn't meant to sound sarcastic. "I'll call you back," she promised, dropping the receiver and making a dash for the front door. Brassy followed at her heels, barking, nearly tripping her.

She pulled open the door, surprising Sheriff Dawson, whose index finger was poised to press the doorbell. He shuffled his big feet around, an apologetic expression on his acne scarred face. Liz's imagination whirled like the earth on its axis. *David or Jessie were in an accident. Fire broke out at the campus. A student went berserk and shot them.*

"Come in," she said, her manners automatic. She felt as limp as the old rag doll Jessie had clung to as a child.

The sheriff removed his hat and nodded his balding head in greeting, but not before he stole a quick glance around the large entranceway of the Pass's mansion. It was quite a layout.

"Is something wrong?" Liz croaked. Her throat was dry as burned toast. "Is it David or Jessie?" It took all the courage she could muster to ask, but she had to know.

"No, it's not them." He wagged his head in response and began twisting his wide-brimmed hat in his hands.

Liz sighed in relief, wilting like a flaccid stalk of celery.

"It's your husband."

"Damon?" She couldn't imagine anything happening to Damon. He was always in control. Invincible.

"Yes. He's in the hospital." The sheriff spat out the words, glad to have the message delivered. Now that the news was in her ballpark, he wondered how she'd react. He hoped she wasn't the hysterical type. He wasn't adept at handling weepy women.

"In the hospital? A heart attack?" Liz guessed, jumping to what seemed a logical conclusion. Damon had been stressed this morning, as he had been for several weeks since he announced his decision to sell the plant. Then yesterday, Mike Rule walked off the job.

"No." The sheriff paused, watching for her reaction. "He was shot."

"How could that be?" Liz scoffed at the very thought. She couldn't assimilate this news.

The sheriff dismissed her question. For one thing, he didn't have an answer. If he did, he'd be as almighty as God. And *that* he wasn't.

"Do you have family here? Somebody to drive you to the hospital?" When she replied with a slight wagging of her head, he took charge. "I'll drive you to the hospital."

She was shocked and in no condition to drive. For her to get behind the wheel would put herself, as well as everyone else on the road, in jeopardy.

She pivoted, flung open the closet door, and pulled out her navy pea coat. Her hands trembled as she plunged her arms into its insulated sleeves.

Dawson admired Mrs. Pass's slender backside as she turned to place the hangar back on the rod. Being neat and organized was habit with her, he guessed. When he saw her hands trembling, he was moved by a wave of sympathy. How would his wife handle news like this?

"I must call my son and daughter. And Cory. But first I need to see Damon so I know what to tell them." Liz spoke aloud, making mental notes for herself. The lump of bread dough resting on the counter would get a long rest. She couldn't care less.

"I'll drive you to the hospital," the sheriff repeated as she fumbled in her purse for her car keys, obviously having forgotten he'd said he'd take her to the hospital. She appeared to be relatively calm, but appearances didn't count when a person was under stress or in shock. Besides, he needed to question her about her activities this morning. She looked innocent enough, but routine dictated that all bases be covered.

Pass had been found approximately forty minutes ago. There was no way she could have made it home between the time her husband was found and when he knocked on her door. He'd broken all the speed limits getting here. And there were no tire tracks in the newly fallen snow.

Besides, they already had a suspect.

Once in the sheriff's car, speeding down the road with the siren going, Liz asked about Damon's condition. She rubbed her head, which suddenly felt as if somebody had whacked her with a jack hammer. "My head is aching. The siren doesn't help," she complained.

"He's in intensive care," he told her, reaching to turn off the siren. "We haven't been allowed to question him. Not yet." He kept his eyes on the road, swinging around the few cars they met. It was fast becoming snow covered and slick. To make conversation, he commented on the weather. "This weather is typical of Michigan," he observed, "but it's still early for snow."

"Who would do such a thing? Who would harm Damon?" Liz cried, not expecting an answer. She opened her purse and searched for a tissue. The news was beginning to sink in now, and tears leaked down her cheeks.

He answered, giving her the bare bones of what he knew as fact. Somebody must have been lying in wait for Damon and had shot him as he stepped out of his car. He didn't tell her any of the gruesome details, specifically that Damon had been shot at close range. Perhaps the gunman wasn't a skilled marksman, or maybe the person wanted to make certain Damon was a goner. He'd failed, but things didn't look good for Pass. He was barely alive and could be headed for surgery at that very moment, unless they needed Mrs. Pass's permission.

"We'll do our best to find the guy," Dawson promised her. "The state crime lab will be called on the scene." That fact was a given.

"Was my husband conscious?" Liz asked. She worried about Damon's denial of faith.

Sheriff Dawson ignored her question. Instead he asked, "Do you live alone? I mean except for your husband?" He knew the Passes had two grown kids, who he was reasonably certain were away, going to some college in the U.P. If Mrs. Pass lived alone, he was concerned about her safety. If this was a grudge crime connected with the plant closing, Mrs. Pass might be in danger. There was heavy speculation that this might be a revenge attack.

He decided against expressing his concern. The office girls who'd arrived for work at eight-thirty said they'd overheard an argument between the accountant and Pass the day before. "Mr. Pass and Mike were shouting so loud we could hear them with the door closed," the one named Sarah had said. She was blatantly frank about her suspicion of Mike Rule.

As the sheriff's car sped down the road, Liz's head spun with questions as she tried to comprehend the horrible facts as far as she knew them.

And to think that only this morning she was feeling sorry for herself, searching for things to do, unhappy with her house, with life in general. Depressed. Now she wished she were back in her kitchen, bored and unhappy. Being bored was far better than racing for the hospital with Damon's life in danger.

After Damon left for work, the house was empty, the silence deafening. As she sipped the last few sips of her morning coffee, she wished once more that she were back in her small home in town. *This is my home, but it doesn't feel at all like home. It's a luxurious house of conveniences that lend creature comforts. But there are few happy memories dwelling within these walls.*

She looked around the kitchen, seeing if she'd overlooked anything that needed her woman's touch. As her eyes drifted over the large kitchen with its cherry cabinets and built-in steel appliances and gadgets, she found it amazing that she lived in this glamorous, four-thousand square foot house that could proudly take its place in the pages of *Better Homes and Gardens*. She'd never dreamed she would live in such a fabulous home, nor had she ever expected to. True, she had often complained to Damon about the lack of closet space in the old house and wished the washer and dryer weren't down in the basement. But now, living here, trapped as it were, she wasn't happy. She felt guilty for not enjoying it as she should.

One day she had complained to Damon, "I feel like a misplaced person living here."

"I'll never understand you," he scolded her. "I worked hard, or you wouldn't have this house. You should consider yourself lucky to have all this!" At the time they had been standing in the family room. He waved his arms around to include the enormous stone fireplace that was his particular pride and joy. He'd personally selected the stones that went into it, working like a convict serving time at hard labor. He'd collected them in a business acquaintance's field.

"I appreciate the house, and I know you worked hard to make it possible, but it doesn't feel like home. Not yet," she'd repeated, hoping to make him understand how she felt.

This new log house had luxuries she had always coveted, space being the number one luxury. And of course, she couldn't deny that she liked the built-in-conveniences. She loved being able to look out and see the woods and, on occasion, wildlife instead of houses, cars, and the voices of distraught neighbors pitched high and clear, regardless of who might overhear. But nothing—space, ample closets, the view, the dream kitchen—compensated for the way she felt about leaving the old neighborhood. Familiar surroundings were comforting somehow. In the old neighborhood, she could walk two doors down and talk to Cory.

"I know how hard you've worked," she repeated, on the verge of tears.

"I doubt it," Damon said, fingering his mustache with the stub of his forefinger. He'd lost his finger in the early years of their marriage when he was first beginning his furniture business.

She didn't push the issue, but she wished she could make him understand this longing within herself, the emptiness, the lack of fulfillment, whatever it was. This discontent was more than a matter of moving from the old house. She felt guilty for feeling as she did. She had everything most women hoped for: grown children with good minds and healthy bodies, this house, her friend Cory, her church, her health. The discontent lay within herself.

She didn't understand herself, so how could she possibly expect Damon to have a clue as to how she felt? On the verge of tears, she had left him standing there and gone to the kitchen on the pretense that she needed to check the roast she'd put in the oven.

"You need to get out of the house. Do something," Cory had lectured.

"Maybe it's just change of life," Liz replied, forcing herself to laugh, wanting to change the subject.

No, she couldn't fault Damon or anybody for the lack of unrest that aggravated her like a missing piece of a puzzle. She was well aware that she alone was accountable for this emptiness. Unhappiness. Whatever it was. *I'm a basket case.*

There seemed to be no purpose in life now that the children were grown. Her restlessness, she supposed, was magnified by empty-nest syndrome. How she had wailed like a baby when they'd dropped Jessie off at college! Damon hadn't said a word of condemnation. Jessie was the apple of his eye.

I never thought I'd miss Jessie's sassy mouth or David's super energy. David had slammed in and out of the house, rushing from one activity to another: football practices, football games, eating on the run, youth group meetings, or over to friends.

A "woof" sounded outside the back door, jarring her out of her reverie. Brassy, her cocker spaniel, was telling her he wanted in. Opening the door, he scampered inside and dashed to sniff his empty dish. "You chow hound," Liz laughed. Detecting no disapproval in her voice, Brassy wagged his cropped tail. He was her dog child.

Sighing deeply, she'd made a conscious effort to push the troubling discontent aside. She needed something to occupy her mind. What could it be? Before the kids went away to college which, pushing the speed limit, was a ten-hour distance, life had been hectic. There had been very little time to dwell on her personal crater of discontent. Every day had been crammed with business, the laundry, cooking meals, appointments to keep, and school events to attend. Those times had been burdensome, but they were some of the best of times, she had decided with the vantage point of good old hindsight.

Now David was in his third year of college and Jessie her first. Time had acted like a short chain when they were still at home, tethering her mind and energy. *I need to find something to do or go berserk. What could I do? Who would hire me? I have no skills. Maybe I should buy a computer, go on line, and chat with strangers as some women do. No, not for me.*

After she'd graduated from high school, she'd worked briefly in an office until she'd met and married Damon, who was her senior by eight years. He was handsome as a young man—still was for that matter. She had been awed by his ambition and his plans for his future. He'd shared more of his private thoughts and ambitions when they dated. Now he told her little about the business, nor had he consulted her about selling Northern Products.

She supposed she was lonely when she met Damon. At the time she was still mourning her parents, who were in their late thirties when she was born, and who died just after she graduated from high school. She sighed again, thinking that it had been natural for her to seek love and security. Damon had filled that gap.

Now she had nearly twenty-five years experience as a wife, the same number of years housekeeping, and twenty-four years as a mom. Cory said she envied the way Liz was so organized. Big deal! Where would that ability get her? Not far in the modern world. Her housewifely skills included baking and sewing. They served to occupy her time, but she rarely sewed now. Anything she needed or wanted, she went out and bought.

Right at the moment she'd welcome a counter full of dishes to wash. Even the chore of cleaning the house, which filled empty spaces in time, had been whisked from her. Damon had insisted they hire a woman to help clean. He'd scold if he knew she worked along with Nora, doing the menial jobs like washing windows and sanitizing their private bath, which she preferred doing herself. Bathrooms revealed personal secrets that weren't anybody's business. Damon didn't like Nora. She didn't know why. Besides, he rarely had occasion to see her. She liked Nora and enjoyed having her company.

Damon, she recognized, controlled her life. Deferring to him had begun when she was a young bride. She'd allowed him to take charge, except for a few matters such as church attendance. He scoffed at "religion," but on Sundays he was usually occupied with some furniture design or tooling machinery. As long as she had Sunday dinner on the table at one o'clock, he didn't complain.

He had been furious when David told them he planned to go into the ministry. "You'll get tired of it soon enough when you've no life of your own, people crying on your shoulder, not a minute to yourself. And not two dimes in your pocket to rub together. I'm sure not paying for your education if you plan on throwing your life away." David didn't argue. He said he'd borrow the money.

It was soon after that disagreement that Damon put the business up for sale. He'd expected David to work with him at the shop and to eventually take over management. *He's punishing himself more than David,* Liz decided, if that had motivated his decision to sell. The business was Damon's life. How could he just up and sell it?

In some respects they were a dysfunctional family. No denying it. The children hadn't suffered notably when they were growing up. But now there was the estrangement between Damon and David. They were cordial with one another, but they avoided any personal interaction.

Jessica was trying her wings, expressing her independence in defiance of all Liz and Damon had tried to impress upon her. The mod clothes she wore resembled something women of ill repute wore when Liz was young. *Girls looked so much prettier and feminine then,* Liz thought. The mod clothing of today was too far out for her taste.

Then this a.m., to fill some time, she had decided to bake bread. As she spread the pastry cloth, she was glad Damon had left the house earlier than usual. He had been in a sour mood this morning. A health nut, he always said breakfast was the most important meal of the day. This morning he refused even a glass of orange juice. She knew then that he was upset. He had grumbled that Mike Rule had quit. Just flat walked off the job! She imagined that having your accountant walk out without any warning would be enough to tie your nerves in knots.

She found it hard to believe that Mike Rule had quit when he had a family to support. He'd be out of work once the business was sold, or whatever the new owner decided, but why resign *now?* He and Damon must have had a major run in, which was hard to imagine. Mike was a placid person from what she'd seen of him. Damon confided very little about the business, so she was pretty much in the dark as to what was transpiring. She learned most of what she knew from reading the local newspaper. That's how she first knew the plant was closing.

"I read in the paper that you're selling the business," she'd charged indignantly, slapping down the newspaper and nearly upsetting her orange juice. They were seated at the breakfast table on a Saturday morning.

Damon looked like he'd bitten into a lemon. "I'm sick of the union," he'd sputtered. She gave up prying when he sarcastically added, "What does it matter to you? We won't be deprived of anything without the business." If she hadn't grown used to having her feelings hurt, she might have cried.

She guessed the employees and the public hadn't a clue that she wasn't Damon's closest confidant. She'd often wondered what Damon planned to do once he retired, and she guessed that nobody, except Cory, would believe that she had only the vaguest idea. He subscribed to numerous travel magazines, but she would be dumfounded if he planned to travel. He'd told her once that when he retired he planned to design and sell patterns for furniture.

She'd never told Damon about the incident in the supermarket. Lacking anything to do, she'd taken a bowl from the cupboard, in preparation for making bread Damon was loath to eat. "It's fattening," he argued, and rightly so, she knew. She didn't indulge in it for that reason. But baking was something she liked to do, and she was good at it. Besides, it filled the time. Thanksgiving was still weeks away, but she'd stick it in the freezer. Jessie and David loved homemade bread. And she could always give a loaf to Cory. Her husband had no qualms about eating bread, fattening or not. "You can sink your teeth into homemade bread," Ben claimed, "and it doesn't turn into a glob of glue in your mouth."

Two deer trotted across the lawn, stopping at the bird feeder to check out the corn beneath it that was intended for the squirrels. It was a peaceful scene. The setting of this house was a tranquil one, but it wasn't enough to keep her from missing the old neighborhood, the old sights and sounds. The kids had grown up there, played with the kids in that neighborhood and still counted some of them as friends. And she missed having Cory close by.

"This house sets me apart from people," Liz once confided to Cory.

"It's not made any difference to me," Cory reasoned, adding honestly, "I'd give my eye teeth to have a house like this."

Those had been her thoughts this morning. She regretted the fact that she and Damon hadn't been on the same page. He wasn't sensitive at all to her feelings. Except in matters that concerned the kids, he'd never included her in his life.

Liz wasn't prepared to see Damon lying in a hospital bed, unconscious and unresponsive. The doctor was waiting her approval to perform surgery. She called Cory.

Cory was at her side within minutes. "I called the pastor," she whispered. "He has a terrible cold and doesn't want to spread the germs around. He said he'll be in touch with the hospital."

"I don't know if Damon would want him here." Liz could be honest with Cory.

David and Jessie made the grueling ten-hour drive from college. They were unprepared to find their father in this grave condition. He hadn't rallied from the anesthetic, and the beep of the monitor was unsettling.

Jessie was inconsolable. "Who would do this to my father?" she cried, tears washing down her smooth young cheeks. "He will get better, won't he?" All Liz could do was hug her. She made no false promises.

At midnight Liz suggested they go home for some rest. " I'll stay with your father."

Reluctantly David agreed. He wanted to be there for his mother, but Jessie's grief was wearing on Liz. He insisted that Jessie go home with him. "Mom will call if Dad wakes up," he reassured her. "And Cory is here."

At five o'clock the next morning, Damon died. He'd regained consciousness and recognized Liz. He gave her a faint smile. "You'll be free now," he whispered. The words were forced as he labored for breath.

"Silly man. I've been free," she whispered a white lie, smiling through tears. Recalling her discontent, the thought flitted through her mind that the opposite was true.

She leaned down and kissed him as a nurse, alerted by the monitor, rushed in.

"Would you like me to say a prayer?" The nurse stood at Damon's bedside, a sweet smile on her face. She had broken hospital policy before.

"Yes," Damon managed to reply through dry, fevered lips.

He died before the nurse could begin.

Chapter Two

ON HER OWN

A week after the funeral, David and Jessie left to return to college. Without them the house seemed to expand until Liz felt as tiny as a star in the universe. The days were lonely, the nights lonelier. She missed the security of Damon's warm body lying beside her. Every noise— the creaking and cracking sounds in and around the house—were sounds she'd ignored before, or had not heard. She lay tense, listening, fearful.

Brassy sensed her uneasiness and followed her to the bedroom door and looked up, watching with unwavering eyes, waiting for an invitation to be invited in. Damon had never allowed the dog in their room, but the thought of Brassy being close by was comforting, even though his snoring sounded like thunder rumbling in a storm. She snapped her fingers and motioning for him to follow her into the bedroom. He raced in, tail wagging, with the speed and agility of a pup. He flopped down beside her bed and stretched out as if he'd always slept there.

She fell asleep and was startled by a sudden movement on the bed, something or someone bouncing up and down. She was terrified. Fear clamped her in its tight fist. Had somebody entered the house? Was she about to be murdered in her bed or raped? But almost as quickly, her sense of smell detected a familiar odor. There was no mistaking Brassy's own peculiar doggy smell. The tension that had tightened every muscle in her body relaxed. As Brassy completed his three circles and flopped down to lie on her feet, she chuckled. "All right, Brassy," she said, patting his head. "You can keep my feet warm." The last thought she had before drifting off to sleep was that she was safe with Brassy on guard. He'd set off a yapping alarm if anybody so much as touched a door.

The next morning she was awake before dawn, thinking of people she must contact and business she must tend to. These spinning thoughts made going back to sleep impossible. Lethargy was replaced by nervous energy.

First she must call Mike Rule, who'd been cleared of all suspicion, to find out if he would meet her at the office and help her sort things out. She had no idea what needed to be done, or whether anything *needed* to be done, until the new owner showed up. If she knew who it was, it would solve a major problem. The business, at least, would be off her hands. Wonderful thought!

She hoped Mike would be willing to help her. She was prepared to offer him any wage he wanted. Mike's wife, children, and close neighbors supported his claim that he'd not left the house the morning Damon was shot. What little she'd seen of Mike, she never thought for a minute he could be guilty. According to news reports, he didn't own a gun of any kind.

Now wrapped comfortably in her worn rose-colored chenille robe, Liz began measuring coffee. She remembered that she needed to make only half as much and was suddenly consumed with self-pity. She hated being alone and dreaded facing the problems concerning the business. She hadn't the vaguest idea of what needed to be done. She guessed that Mike Rule would be a great help if he'd agree to work for her. She was about to pour herself a cup of the fresh brew when she decided to call Mike now, before she did another thing. It would be a relief to know his answer, even if it wasn't the one she hoped for.

She picked up the receiver and was preparing to punch in the number when the phone rang, startling her. The man's voice on the line wasn't familiar, "Mrs. Pass?"

Her first thought was to hang up. The murderer was still at large, free as a bird.

"Mrs. Pass?" the man inquired again. "This is Tom Kelley."

"Kelley?"

"Yes, Tom Kelley. I'm the one who purchased your husband's business. I've tried to reach him at the plant, but no one answers. I'm in town and thought I'd stop in and see him."

"Oh! You haven't heard what—what happened?" One hand clutched her throat..

"No, I was living downstate, almost to the Ohio border. Then I took a vacation in the wilderness of Canada. No phones. Nothing. Just trees. Is there something I should know?"

"Yes, there is." She hadn't needed to tell anybody that Damon had been murdered, and she dreaded repeating the story to a stranger. It made his death more horrible, if that were possible. Fighting an urge to cry, she managed to go on. "My husband died a little over a week ago. He was shot." Saying he was shot was easier to say than he was murdered.

"I'm so sorry. I didn't know, or I wouldn't have called you. I know my lawyer has been trying to reach me. I was going to call him today. Is there someone else I might talk to?" His voice conveyed genuine sympathy.

Hoping to collect herself, and with receiver in hand, Liz walked to the counter where the coffee pot squatted and poured herself a cup. Her hands were shaking so that coffee splashed on the tile floor. She'd scold the kids if they were that careless.

"I was about to get in touch with the accountant who worked for my husband. I know nothing about the business." She felt like such an ignoramus, and to her dismay, her words had turned into a whine.

"If you have the accountant's phone number, I'll call him," Kelley assured her. His voice had a calming affect. "I'd like to meet him and get things going. Your husband and I had the business end of the sale settled. I imagine I can take over without any paperwork."

Liz felt as though a huge weight were being lifted from her shoulders. She wasn't a scholar of the Bible, but she remembered a verse that referred to Jesus carrying burdens with a person. Was God truly involved and caring for her? It was a reassuring thought.

"I can meet you at the plant if I know what time you are going to be there. Mr. Rule doesn't have a key." Damon had never trusted anybody with a key, even Mike Rule. She did know that much. "I hope Mr. Rule can help you," she added.

"I hope so, too. It would make the transition easier. Could you meet me at the plant around ten? Does that give you enough time?"

Rushing to take a shower, Liz hoped the police tape surrounding the back entrance at the plant was down. She hadn't driven around there to know, because she simply didn't want to. The plant hadn't been broken into. The only thing missing had been the money from Damon's wallet, which the police found on the ground beside his wounded body.

Arriving at the plant, Liz recognized Mike Rule sitting in his beat-up, yellow Ford pickup. Apparently he had agreed to meet Tom Kelley at the plant. No doubt he would be relieved to get his old job back, providing he wanted to work for Mr. Kelley. A stranger in a dark green SUV was parked next to him. She supposed it was Kelley.

Kelley jumped out of his vehicle the moment he saw Liz pull in and rushed to open her car door. She hadn't been shown that kind of respect in ages, she thought, feeling a trifle embarrassed by this courtesy.

"You must be Mrs. Pass." He smiled.

"And you must be Mr. Kelley," she returned, thinking that he certainly looked trustworthy, if looks could be translated as trust.

As they walked up the steps leading to Damon's office, she observed that he was clean- shaven and casually dressed. His brown leather jacket fit him perfectly without creasing at the waistline, which indicated the absence of 'love handles.'

The two of them exchanged comments about the weather, as strangers do when it is the only topic they have in common. Even so, Tom Kelley exuded an air of relaxed self-confidence without being arrogant. With his easy smile and masculine good looks, Liz supposed he didn't have trouble making friends. He towered over her by at least five inches, so she had to look up at him. It was somehow disconcerting. And she was wearing dress boots with heels! His perfect posture was the one thing that reminded her of Damon. *Will I always compare every man to Damon?*

Once inside, with Mike dragging behind, they explored the plant and the office. "I've decided to keep the plant running as it is. Manufacturing furniture, I mean," Kelley explained.

"The business has been making a fair profit," Mike interjected. "I don't know why Damon wanted to sell."

Both men looked to Liz for an explanation. "I haven't the faintest idea." She shrugged. "I never signed any sales agreement or contract, so I assume my name wasn't on it as an owner. In fact, I didn't know for certain the sale was completed."

"The business end is completed. " Tom Kelley looked puzzled.

"All I know is that a large deposit was made to our bank account. Damon must have had plans to invest it in stock, or whatever. I have no idea." Perplexed, Liz shrugged her slim shoulders.

"That's all that matters." Tom Kelley hurried to correct himself. "I mean, I'm happy for you that there is no problem about getting what is rightfully yours." Liz's confusion tugged at his heart.

"Did you tell Mr. Pass that you intended to keep the furniture business going?" Mike asked. His curiosity had got the best of him. He had to know.

"I thought at first I might turn it into a paper mill, but I changed my mind. It seemed foolish to go to the expense of changing over when the business was profitable. And the timber here is suited for making furniture. It would be a shame to pulverize it for paper. I believe I told him so." Tom Kelley looked thoughtful as he contemplated Mike's question.

"He sure put on an act, letting all of us think we'd be out of jobs!" Mike stormed.

Kelley's eyebrows shot up, but he let the remark pass. Liz liked him better for this tactful thoughtfulness. Nevertheless, she was embarrassed by Mike's remark. It put Damon in a poor light and reflected on him as a person. At the same time, she understood where Mike was coming from. Why had Damon been so secretive?

"I'm so relieved everything is settled." She heaved a sigh of relief.

Kelley grinned spontaneously, feeling happy for her.

"Why don't we all go to lunch and get acquainted?" Kelley asked then, turning to get Liz's answer. He expected Mike to go since he was familiar with how the business operated. "We can talk while we eat."

They lunched at a nearby mom and pop restaurant. Liz felt uncomfortable. She didn't feel she was really needed for discussing the business, but Tom Kelley soon put her at ease. He asked about the children and if she had any plans now that she was alone.

"Not at this point," she told him, regretting that she didn't have some great plan with which to impress him. "All I know how to do is to keep house, and I have no desire to hire out." She laughed at her own joke.

Kelley laughed in appreciation of her humor in light of the recent tragedy she had experienced. "I saw a file marked 'personal' in the main office. You might look through it at your leisure."

"I can do that, Mr. Kelley," she told him. "I'm busy this afternoon, getting death certificates—that kind of thing." Then she added, "I think the local newspaper, *Northern Times,* should be notified of your intention to keep the plant open."

"You're right. I want to announce the reopening of the plant, and I need the employees to report to work. I'll let the newspaper know exactly when," Kelley said.

Liz's self-confidence was elevated a notch. She had been able to offer some viable input after all.

"Mr. Kelley is so formal. I'd rather you called me Tom. Both of you," he said, turning to look first at Liz and then at Mike.

"And I'm Liz," she quickly returned.

After ordering, they touched briefly on the subject of Damon's death. "Do the police have any leads about who was responsible for your husband's death?" Tom wondered aloud.

"Not to my knowledge. They are clueless, but they think it might have been someone with a grudge over the plant closing."

"I see." Tom shook his head, a scowl on his face. "How cold-hearted some people are. I am so sorry about your loss." His face was tender with sympathy for Liz.

The waitress brought their order of sandwiches. Liz had lifted her BLT and was about to take a bite when Tom asked, "Shall I say grace?"

Liz and Mike, both caught off-guard, nodded their agreement. The simple prayer of thanks Tom Kelley offered up moved Liz. Hearing a man other than a pastor say a prayer was new to her.

Mike reacted by exclaiming, "Mr. Kelley, now I *know* I want to work for you!"

Liz drove up her long, curved, gravel driveway that she intended to have paved next spring. Gus had been on the job again. The driveway was clear of snow, and he'd removed it.

Inside, she slipped off her coat and boots and walked to the family room with Brassy following at her heels. Each step she took on the parquet floor echoed through the house, stamping upon her mind and heart that she was truly alone. She settled into her favorite chair beside a fireplace that had no fire and was full of ashes. It left her feeling chilled, a chill that went deeper than the room's temperature.

Removing the ashes was one job Nora hadn't been assigned. Damon had insisted on doing it himself. He worried that she wouldn't open the flue before she began. Now she had no intention of asking Nora to do the dirty job. It would give her something to do besides thinking about herself.

Looking around, she said aloud, "So now what do I do, living in this enormous house?" Brassy, who had flopped down at her feet, lifted his head and gazed up at her. Sensing that no command had been given, he dropped his head on his paws and stared up at her, brown eyes unblinking. "I know you don't know the answer," she said, leaning down to give him a reassuring pat, "even if you could talk."

The old feeling of restlessness claimed her, dragging at her spirits. *I could go off on a cruise, go to Europe—preferably France—buy myself a new wardrobe,* she thought, playing with a list of possibilities. *Or I could rent an apartment near the campus. Then I'd be near the kids. Wouldn't they love that!* She chuckled at this ridiculous idea. *But I don't want any of those things. Not now, anyway. I have everything material any woman could want. So what do I want?*

A silly thought popped into her head. How guilty it made her feel! If she met a man like Tom Kelley, she'd want to get married again. There was a magnetism about him that appealed to her, and obviously he was a Christian. Being a Christian hadn't been a priority for a husband when she'd married Damon. But from experience she knew now what the Bible meant by being unequally yoked.

Foolish woman, she lectured herself, *you don't need a man to keep you happy.* On the other hand, there was certainly nothing wrong with becoming friends with a person of the opposite sex. Unless he—Tom specifically—was married. Sooner or later she'd find out his marital status, perhaps when she went to the plant the next week.

Chapter Three

THE COMMITMENT

More than two weeks had passed since Damon's death, and Sunday faithfully rolled around once again. Liz wanted to pull the covers over her head and sleep the day away. Normally she wasn't a person to lie in bed. Now her body felt weighted down as if she were covered with a lead blanket. The holidays, when David and Jessie would come home for Thanksgiving, were several weeks away. There was nothing to look forward to. Gloomy, depressing thought. If it hadn't been for habit, she would have given in to depression. But habit prevailed, saving her from herself. She knew that if she didn't show up at church, Cory would drive over and lecture her. With a long, weary sigh, she shoved the covers aside—Brassy along with them—and slid out of bed.

"I'm on automatic pilot," she said to Brassy as she fell into her familiar Sunday routine. She showered, dressed, and fed Brassy. Not feeling like eating a more substantial breakfast, she warmed some leftover coffee from the evening before and drank a glass of juice. Then she headed out for church, her heart as heavy as a child's without a Christmas tree.

At church, people nodded perfunctory greetings. A few women gave her gentle, warm hugs, but they quickly parted, opening a path for her to proceed into the sanctuary. In spite of being wrapped in the warmth of her new black wool coat, she shivered. The mechanical encounters were like something given to a newcomer, someone who didn't really belong here. She wished she hadn't come.

"You're being ridiculous," she lectured herself. She'd attended this church since the kids were born, over twenty years ago. *If I feel like an outsider, I have no one to blame but myself.* She acknowledged that fact now. She had never made an effort to get involved in the programs of the church or the Bible studies or the women's society. The kids had loved it here, had friends here that were like family, and had been active in youth activities.

She was tempted to fix the blame for her lack of involvement on Damon. He had heckled her about going to church, accusing her of needing a crutch. Now, looking back, she knew she had been so insecure in her faith that she fell prey to his verbal accusations. Except for Sunday worship, she'd made excuses for not accepting invitations to the functions of the church. Damon had ruled her life. There was no denying it. Still, she missed him and had loved him, warts and all. Her eyes misted in sympathy for Damon and for herself.

Now she was free to do as she pleased, each and every day, each and every moment. The knowledge was gratifying, like a gift. Unfortunately, the gift came wrapped in the baggage of guilty feelings. She deeply regretted that it was Damon's horrifying death that had freed her. However, the question remained. She was free to do *what?* She asked herself that question again as she took a seat in her usual pew halfway down the aisle.

Besides feeling guilty, she felt vulnerable as a child without any defenses. Damon had been her security, standing between her and the world as a defender against all dangers. She gave him credit for taking care of numerous problems, like replacing fuses in the switch box or changing the oil in the car, simply giving her a feeling of security by his presence. In her heart she valued his loyalty and respected his memory for it. Their marriage had been a partnership in ways that counted for more than she realized until now.

Shortly after she settled herself, Cory slid in beside her, accompanied by her husband Ben. *Yes,* she thought, *I've never been entirely alone here. There's always Cory, shoring me up.* She squeezed Cory's hand and smiled, grateful for the support of this wonderful friend.

As the service progressed, Liz focused on the minister's sermon. At the same time, she was aware of those seated in the rows ahead of her. While she didn't know most of the people in church personally, she could sort the regulars from the visitors. She spotted June Davidson from the office, who had attended Damon's memorial service. Sarah never showed. She needed to contact both women about returning to work as a favor to Mr. Kelley. Or Tom, as he had insisted on being called.

Seated two rows ahead, one head stood out from the rest, catching her attention. The thick, wavy hair rang a bell. When the man turned to the woman beside him, perhaps to get her reaction to a remark of the pastor's, Liz recognized him instantly. It was none other than Tom Kelley! It was perfectly obvious that the woman, whom she didn't recognize as a regular attendee, was someone of whom Tom was fond. She could tell by the way his face crinkled into a smile when he turned to look at her.

She wasn't surprised to see Kelley at church. From his demeanor and his prayer when they ate lunch, she knew he was a Christian. She sighed, telling herself to be thankful that he was a Christian. In the next few days, out of necessity, she would have more occasions to meet with him. She'd be spared the vulgar language and suggestive remarks some men delighted in.

Taking a pencil from the cardholder on the back of the pew in front of her, she scribbled a note on her bulletin and nudged Cory. Cory scanned the note. Taking the pencil from Liz, she scribbled a reply: *He's a looker. Does he have relatives here? Is that his wife?*

Liz shrugged, took the pencil back, and jotted a reply: *I don't know. I suppose she's his wife.* Ben leaned slightly forward, his eyebrows scrunched together in a good-natured scowl. Cory and Liz smiled like children caught with their hands in a cookie jar. Ben smiled at them and gently took Cory's hand in his. Liz, while rejoicing for Cory, felt a pang of jealousy. Cory was blessed to have a husband like Ben.

The minister's message urged Christians to use their talents and abilities—whatever resources they had at their disposal—to further the kingdom of God. "Commit yourselves to some service for the Lord, and know the joy of doing something worthwhile," he implored them.

Liz decided the message did not apply to her. She wasn't a mover or a shaker and lacked any talents. God was not putting the finger on her, expecting anything spectacular in the way of changing the world or of making even a small dent. She was a nobody, with nothing to offer. Nevertheless, she felt a response stirring within. The trauma of Damon's death had awakened her to her own spiritual poverty. She needed to put away childish ways, like feeling sorry for herself. *What I've worshipped as God was but the hem of His garment,* she acknowledged to herself.

As the sermon progressed to point three, the pastor listed a number of needs of people living in their town. He told of a young woman who needed a place to live. "Only temporarily," he hastened to add.

Thoughts of her spacious house made her squirm. Only yesterday she had told Cory, "The house is so quiet, I can hear the dust fall."

The idea of having someone living with her in her huge house was appealing. Liz pushed aside the negative questions that exploded in her mind like yeast in bread. It was definite. Yes, she would talk to the pastor after the service and ask him about the girl and her situation. Offering the girl a place to stay was something she could do, a commitment she could make without really sacrificing too much. And she selfishly admitted, she'd benefit as much as the young woman. She could say good-bye to constant loneliness.

"Come to dinner with us." Cory extended the invitation as they were making their way to the front entrance of the sanctuary, where the pastor stood shaking people's hands. "I have a pot roast in the oven."

"Sounds great. Did you hear my stomach growling? How embarrassing. But first I want to talk to the pastor."

Cory gave her a quizzical look. Was Liz holding out on her? "What's going on?"

"Tell you about it later," Liz put her off. "At your house."

As she waited for the congregation to file out, she saw Tom Kelley approaching. It was perfectly childish, she knew, but she stepped back, hoping to avoid him. Shyness she hadn't experienced since she was a young woman made her feel self-conscious. She was certain her timidity was written on her face as clearly as the Ten Commandments were written on stone tablets. But no such luck! He spotted her as he looked around, taking in the layout and decor of the church.

"Mrs. Pass." He addressed her formally, she thought, because of the people around them. But there was no mistaking his pleasure at seeing her. His face lit up, and his dark eyes shone. "I will see you at the office tomorrow, won't I?"

"Yes." A smile spread across her face. She waited expectantly for him to introduce his wife, but he moved ahead, apparently being sensitive to the people waiting to shake the pastor's hand.

The pastor was pleased by Liz's offer to take in the young woman. "Come to the parsonage this afternoon. I'll introduce you to Mary. She's been staying temporarily with us. I believe you'll like her."

Chapter Four

HOUSE GUEST

"You're taking in a total stranger." Cory screwed up her face in disbelief when Liz told her she might have a young woman living with her.

"It's not a sure thing yet. I'm meeting her this afternoon. I rather like the idea of having someone living with me. I'd be doing something for somebody, too."

"Who is this girl? Doesn't she have a family? Has she been in trouble? You may be taking in a tough character with all kinds of bad habits." Cory was all skepticism.

Later in the afternoon when Liz met Mary Hartley, she was immediately charmed. The woman, as the pastor had referred to her, was a girl of twenty-one. She was taller than Liz and a trifle overweight. Liz was impressed with her good manners, or social skills as Jessie had labeled a person's ability to relate to others.

When the pastor introduced them, Mary sprang from her seat on the sofa and extended her hand to shake. *Are my kids this respectful?* Liz wondered.

After introductions, Pastor Woods told them he had an emergency call to make. "You two can talk. If you need Mrs. Woods for any reason, don't hesitate. She'll be glad to help. She's in the kitchen, you know," he said, excusing himself.

Once he was gone Mary became apologetic. "Thank you for talking to me. It's a lot to ask of anybody." Her lips were compressed in a smile. Liz had observed earlier that her teeth were out of alignment. Mary was self-conscious about them, she guessed.

"I'm married," Mary told her. Her wide green eyes were beginning to cloud up. "My husband is in Marine boot camp at Parris Island, South Carolina. You've probably heard of it."

Liz nodded, encouraging her to go on.

"I'm not certain where he'll be stationed after he gets through basic training. We're hoping he can get into some specialty training. In the meantime, my grandmother needs me. She's at the nursing home here in town. She's not expected to live long. My mom works, so she isn't able to visit grandma or care for her as she would like to." Mary's eyes flooded, and she searched the pocket of her faded jeans for a tissue. She struggled with her story. Liz nodded her head from time to time to show that she was interested and was listening.

"Mom and Dad live down in Detroit. They moved there after they were married. Dad got work at the Ford plant. I lived there my whole life until now. That's about it, Mrs. Pass."

"So you're here temporarily?" Liz asked.

"Yes, until Brad graduates from boot camp. As I said before, he hopes to get some specialty training. Anything to keep him out of the war. Once he graduates, I'll go wherever he's stationed—unless he gets shipped overseas, like to Iraq. I can't even think about that!" Mary swept one hand across her forehead as she talked. "I wouldn't live with you too long. I'll be here until Brad graduates, or until something happens to Grandma. Then I'd go back and live with my parents."

"You visit your grandma every day?" Liz asked, mentally picturing Mary hanging around the house. Liz's time would revolve around Mary's to some degree, she expected. She must be explicit about details such as Mary's laundry, taking care of her room, and telephone bills. She didn't want to burden Nora with extra work. And how would she get back and forth to visit her grandmother?

"I visit Grandma every chance I get. I have a car," Mary hastened to add as if reading Liz's mind. "It was Brad's before we got married. It's a rust bucket, but it gets me where I'm going."

Glad for the opening, Liz spoke boldly. She offered her the use of her washer and dryer. "I'll respect the privacy of your room. I'll leave the chore of cleaning it up to you."

"I'll certainly do that," Mary quickly agreed, nervously pulling at her sweatshirt. "I'd like to find work, but most places don't want to hire anybody they know will be temporary help."

"Perhaps I can help you there," Liz offered quickly. As soon as the words were out of her mouth, she wished she hadn't been so impulsive. *Now, exactly how do you think you can help?*

"I appreciate this so much. I hope it's not too much of an imposition. I mean, my living at your house. You're sure you have room?" Mary asked.

Liz smiled. "I have enough room." Looking at a picture of Pastor and Mrs. Woods on the end table beside her, she told Mary about Damon.

"You may not know that my husband died recently."

Mary's face fell. She spoke the only words she knew to say, "I'm sorry."

She didn't tell Mary how Damon had died. It was hard to talk about, and she didn't want to frighten her off. She justified her decision by reasoning that Mary might think she'd be morbid company. She did tell Mary, "I'll be busy for a few days helping to clear out my husband's personal things from his office."

"We'll both be going our separate way." Mary said, smiling her closed-mouth smile, obviously relieved. *I'm not expected to be a constant companion.*

"You can follow me home now, unless you prefer to wait until morning. Perhaps you want to give this some thought?" It wasn't Liz's intent to pressure the girl into making a snap decision.

"I need to load my things, and I'll be ready. I didn't bring anything except my clothes."

Once Liz had parked her car in the garage, and Mary pulled in next to her as Liz had instructed, Mary exclaimed as she shut her car door, "I didn't expect to live in a mansion!"

Opening the door leading from the garage into the back entranceway, Liz chuckled. "It's not exactly a mansion. It certainly is more than I need. This is Brassy," she hurried to explain as the dog charged from inside the house to welcome Liz home. "I hope you don't mind having a dog around."

"I love animals," Mary said, dropping her bags and stooping to coax Brassy to come to her. Brassy responded with a quick, sloppy kiss on Mary's cheek.

Liz led Mary through the house and up the broad staircase to one of the spare bedrooms, seeing it through Mary's eyes as she exclaimed over the immensity of the house. Helping Mary lug the suitcases upstairs left her winded. She plopped down on the chintz-covered chair positioned by the north window.

Looking down, she saw a figure walking towards the woods, carrying—what was it? A gun perhaps? In the faint light of dusk, it was difficult to see. "Oh!" She gasped, her heart palpitating, her hands holding her cheeks as if she had a toothache.

"What's wrong?" Mary asked.

"There's somebody down there, going into the woods. Mary, I haven't been fair with you. I'm so sorry." The words jumped from Liz's mouth like corn in a popper.

Puzzled, Mary rushed to look out the window in time to see a man disappear into the woods. "What are you talking about?" she asked, her brows pinching together.

"I should have told you. My husband was killed. Murdered. I have been selfish. I liked the idea of somebody living with me. I don't think I am in any danger." The words poured out like hot syrup. "The police believe the murder was done out of spite. My husband sold the furniture plant, and the employees thought they'd be out of jobs."

"I remember reading about it in the newspapers," Mary recalled.

"If you don't want to stay, I understand," Liz cried, mortified and repentant.

"You don't know for sure that you're in danger." Mary tried to be reassuring. To herself she thought, *She needs me.* To Liz she said, "I'm here. I'll stay."

"I'm glad, Mary. That is kind of you." Liz dabbed at tears threatening to develop into a real crying jag. Mary was a gem, one of God's sparkling jewels.

"Do you think you should call the police?"

"Sheriff Dawson said not to hesitate to call," Liz nodded, picking up the phone from the nightstand. Pausing, one hand hovering above the receiver, she said, "I hope he doesn't think I'm over reacting, but I don't care. I'll call, no matter what he might think."

Sheriff Dawson searched around outside the house. Then accompanied by a deputy, he followed the footprints in the snow leading into the woods. He came back soon and reported that it was Gus Simpson. "He was sitting in his deer blind with his bow. Bow season has started, you know. He said he knew you didn't mind if he hunted on your property." The sheriff paused, grinning, "I did tell him it's six o'clock, and it's unlawful to hunt after dark. It's dark back in the woods now."

Later as she shoved Brassy aside and climbed into bed, Liz thanked God for bringing Mary into her life. The girl was so sensible. As for herself, she had already gained more than she'd given in inviting her to live here. As she tossed and turned, she wondered if Mary understood there was the possibility of danger in living with her. It was an hour or more before she fell asleep. Then she slept like a baby, resting as she hadn't done since Damon's death.

Chapter Five

THE LETTERS

Liz took extra care in applying her makeup and arranging her hair the next morning. Her naturally wavy hair needed a trim, she saw as she turned her head from side to side, peering critically at her reflection in the vanity mirror. Looking her best always gave her more confidence. She'd need all the self-confidence she could muster this morning, she thought. Going to the office and helping out in whatever way she could wasn't a job she relished. She would feel like a fish out of water. But her only job, she guessed, was to go through Damon's private file and sort out what was pertinent to the business and to remove any of his private papers. She wished she could bring the file cabinet home. She'd be more comfortable on her own turf, but Tom Kelley might consider it his property. Resigned, she sighed. Her only option was to go and get the job done. Besides, Kelley trusted her, which was flattering.

Going to the kitchen, she let Brassy out for his morning routine of sniffing around until he found the right tree to water. Then she could begin thinking about breakfast for herself and Mary. They hadn't talked about "rise and shine time" or whether they'd eat breakfast together. Then she heard Mary bounding down the stairs. How much more lively things were with another person in the house!

Mary walked into the kitchen dressed in jeans and a sweatshirt that advertised, *Marines*, ready for the day. *The girl isn't a sluggard,* Liz was thinking as Mary gave her a dazzling smile along with a cheerful, "Good morning!" For that split second Mary had forgotten her crooked teeth.

Having someone to eat with was like a ray of sunshine on a gloomy day. She was ravenous. Her stomach growled in anticipation. This morning she wouldn't need to force herself to eat. If she didn't watch herself, she'd wolf down her food like Brassy did.

"I'm having a boiled egg and a banana. Maybe a slice of toast. How does that sound to you?" she asked, turning to Mary.

Mary giggled in guilty embarrassment. "I usually eat a roll, and that's about all. But what you're having sounds good."

Aha, Liz mused. So now I know why she's overweight. Mary had offered to share the cost of food, but Liz assured her, "Absolutely not. You are my guest."

"I don't know much about cooking," Mary admitted, watching as Liz removed the toaster from its private storage place on the cabinet top. "Mom doesn't do much cooking either, the way she works and all. Most of the time she orders take-out for dinner. Where are the silverware and plates? I'll set the table."

"On the shelf and in that drawer." Liz motioned while she held a pan under the faucet. "I've never worked out, and I enjoy cooking. I love cinnamon rolls and occasionally make a pan when I bake bread. Cinnamon roles are just bread dough with raisins and cinnamon added. And frosting, of course. That's what makes them so delicious. So I don't indulge too often."

"Sounds scrumptious. My mouth is watering just talking about them."

"I'll make a pan the next time I bake bread," Liz promised.

Our first day is off to a good start, Liz thought. *I hope the day at the office goes half as well.*

Tom Kelley was waiting for Liz in his SUV. He appeared relaxed and eager to get to work. She'd not remembered to give him or Mike a key. *Am I preoccupied or absent-minded?* She would call a locksmith, have more keys made, and have the locks changed—whatever Tom decided. That was something she could do today.

Mike was standing at the door, waiting to get in. She apologized for her oversight, and the three of them entered the building. "It sounds hollow in here without the machines running," Mike said. "The silence is deafening, as the saying goes."

"We need to get things up and running ASAP," Kelley said, matter-of-factly.

"I called the paper this morning and told them you are the new owner. They want to interview you, Mr. Kelley," said Liz.

"What's with the 'Mr. Kelley' business? I thought we'd decided on first names."

"Yes, we did," Liz said, blushing. She hoped he thought it was a hot flash. Waving a hand back and forth in front of her face, she said, "It's stuffy in here. Maybe from being closed up." She removed her plaid jacket to give her remark credence. *Oh, the games we play to cover our little sins.*

"I enjoyed the service yesterday," Tom commented. They were standing in the middle of Damon's office, the door hanging open. Without making an issue of it, he stepped over and took down the "Close Door" sign.

"The pastor's messages are always…ah…meaty." She was at loss for a better word.

"My sister goes there, has for years. She was with me on Sunday. Maybe you know her? Maggie Kelley? She never married."

"She's your sister!" Liz fairly crowed. Then, to cover her embarrassment, she blundered on. "No, I don't remember seeing her in church before."

"She attends the earlier service. She only went to the eleven o'clock for my benefit, I think," he speculated. "I'm only staying with her until I find a house of my own. Or until she gets tired of me and kicks me out." He laughed, knowing Maggie loved to have him around.

He still hadn't made mention of a wife, Liz noted. "Living alone does get lonely," she said.

"I am sorry about your husband's death," he repeated the sentiment he'd offered before.

"It was a shock and a hard loss to deal with. I'm still dealing with it."

"I know you must be. I want you to know that I appreciate your willingness to sort things out here. This can't be easy."

"It helps to keep busy, and I know you want to get things organized here."

"Mike, I see, is eager to get to work. He and I will go down to his office. If you need us, you know where to find us."

With little sense of anticipation or curiosity, Liz walked to Damon's personal file, expecting the contents to be boring. Although Damon had confided little about the affairs of the business, she felt there were no surprises in store for her. After all, she'd lived with the man for years and was positive he didn't have any deep secrets.

The first drawer contained letters from Jessie and David, a big surprise. She hadn't guessed Damon was that sentimental, but he had loved the kids. No doubt about it. Keeping their letters was additional proof of that fact. To her surprise, however, she found mail to him they'd addressed to the plant rather than to their home address. She guessed that knowing Damon often worked late, they sent mail here. As she shuffled through the envelopes, she saw by the postmarks that David's correspondence had dwindled since the argument over his career choice. Now she knew why they addressed their letters to her when they sent them home. Putting the letters in one of the boxes she thought to bring along, she decided she would keep the letters for the kids. *I'd love to read them, but that would be downright snoopy of me.*

At the back of that same drawer, bound together by a strong rubber band, were cards she had given Damon on birthdays, anniversaries, and holidays. She wiped at tears with the back of her hand as she reread the trite messages they carried. When she'd selected

The Letters

a card for him, she avoided anything too sentimental, sentiments she didn't feel sincerely in her heart. She'd never been a hypocrite! Now she regretted her hardheartedness. Damon had cherished the cards she'd given him. Amazing discovery. Too late to remedy.

A small packet of letters she took from the next drawer bore unfamiliar handwriting.

They must pertain to the business, she thought. There were no envelopes and no return addresses. Unfolding the first one penned on a ruled sheet of paper, her interest was piqued by the lack of greeting—formal or otherwise. "Damon," the letter began without any pretense of being cordial.

Her imagination began spinning sordid tales. She'd heard too many stories about widows who discovered their deceased husbands had lived dual lives. Had there been another woman in Damon's life? Ludicrous thought! He hardly had time for another woman. Besides, she'd just seen proof that Damon cared enough about her to save her cards.

Caught up in curiosity, she scanned the letter's brief message. From the first line, it carried a tone as smarting as a slap on the face.

"*I'm locked up while you're out there making money and living like a king. You should be in here too. The least you could do is send me some cash, or write. My time in this hole is up in five years. You can bet I'll see you then.*"

The signature was difficult to read. She shifted in her chair so she could read the name in a better light. It appeared to be *Terry*. Who was this ominous man? It was enough to send chills chasing one another up and down her spine. What had Damon done that somebody hated him so? If she hadn't seen the note, she never would have believed it. Lots of people disliked him, but not to this extent.

A knock rapped on the office door. Being absorbed, she jumped. "Come in," she called.

The door swung open, and Tom Kelley poked his head in. "We're taking a break. Want to join us? Mike made some coffee."

"I don't know," She answered dully. Her mind bulged with questions about the letters.

"We will bring you a cup if you prefer," Tom said, disappointed. He'd anticipated her joining them. He wanted to get to know her better.

She gave the file drawer a shove so that it slammed shut. "It sounds good. Thanks." She pushed her chair away from the file, returned to the present world, and stood up. She knew chivalry wasn't dead when Tom opened the door and stood waiting for her to pass through.

The three of them sat cozily around a small table in the tiny cubicle set up for employees to use on their breaks. A window looked out on the parking lot that extended to the rear of the building. She had never been in this room before. *It's like looking into a small slice of Damon's life, if he took his breaks here. Oh Damon, why didn't you include me in your life?*

The men waited on her. She felt like royalty. Tom poured her coffee. Mike located the sugar and powdered cream, explaining that's all there was. "No problem. I drink mine black." She smiled and waved a perfectly groomed hand.

"We're making progress. I don't have any need to worry, not with Mike in charge. He's done an admirable job."

Mike's round face glowed, and he spilled coffee on his pants. He wasn't accustomed to being praised on the job.

"I'm glad you're finding things in order," Liz said. "It's been an eye-opener for me too." She filled them in on the letters from the kids she'd found. At this point she wasn't ready to tell them—or anybody—about the letters from the stranger named Terry. It might only throw a poor light on Damon. His reputation was marred enough. The pastor had once commented that a criticism of your spouse was a judgment on yourself. "You chose that person, and it's a reflection on you if you made the wrong choice." She'd adhered to that homily, except when talking to Cory.

"My wife is happy that I can keep this job. We had T-bone steaks for dinner last evening to celebrate. And she had her hair done. Dark brown this time. I like it. Better than the blonde," Mike rambled on, grabbing a napkin to scrub at his pants. With an effort, he bent down to wipe the spills on the tiled floor.

"My wife had pretty brown hair," Tom volunteered, passing a hand over his face.

"What color is it now?" Mike asked, happy that his new boss acted like a human being.

"Martha passed away three years ago," Tom told them, flashing Mike a forgiving smile for his blunder. "Diabetes," he said, his eyes downcast.

He isn't married. Liz's heart lurched with expectation. But in view of her private thoughts, she was humbled by the awareness of how his wife had died. Diabetes was a terrible disease. Tom must have suffered as he watched his wife struggle against the odds.

Tom turned to look at Liz. "I know something of what you're going through. My wife's illness and death, and then being alone, has opened my eyes to how precious life is. It's been a test of my faith."

"Yes," she said, nodding her head in understanding. "My faith was pretty shallow, but it was a comfort. Damon's death jolted me into seeing I need to be closer to God. And now I'm not alone." Pausing briefly, she went on, "Remember the young woman the pastor told us about on Sunday? She's living with me."

"Really! That's quite an undertaking. I hope it works out for you."

"She'd like to find work." The impact of what she'd just said struck her. She hadn't meant to hint, but he picked up on it without missing a beat.

"Maybe we can do something about it," Tom offered. "What kind of work can she do?"

"I have no idea. I really didn't mean to hint."

"I'd like to help if I can."

"Come over and meet her." Liz was appalled at her own audacity. "Or, I'm sure she'd come here for an interview," she hastened to add.

"I'm not busy tomorrow evening. If you're not busy?"

It was arranged that Tom would be at Liz's the following evening about eight.

Liz returned to Damon's office and to the mysterious letters. If only there were envelopes, she might know the man's last name, or which prison he was in.

She was less than enthusiastic as she pulled the file drawer open and drew out the next letter. From the scribbled date, she knew it had been written three and a half years ago. A quick glance told her it was from the same man. At least the same scrolled hand writing indicated it was he. Checking the signature, it was definitely *Terry*. She wondered if Damon had responded to any of this Terry's letters.

She cast around in her memory, trying to recall if Damon had ever spoken of Terry. She vaguely recalled him telling her that a Terry had been a best friend in high school. At the time she'd been flipping through Damon's senior-high class book, and her eyes had been drawn to a picture with an autograph beside it. "Your best bud, Terry." Terry's outstanding feature was a prominent square jaw.

The tone of the last note was so ominous that her head began throbbing. She felt sick to her stomach. Her only comfort lay in the fact that it was written over three years ago. Her hands were trembling so that she had difficulty slipping the next letter from the packet. It was dated only a year ago:

Damon, old pal, how come you don't answer my letters? Remember what I said about checking out your wife and kids? I keep my word. I'll need some cash when I get out of here. The few bucks they give us won't be enough to keep me in cigarettes and beer.

Terry

There were three more letters, but her nerves were shattered. She couldn't handle reading any more of these chilling messages. Her hands shook as she wrapped the rubber band around them. She had to get out of this office. As she was shoving back her chair, a terrible thought immobilized her. Jessie and David might be in danger. So might she. Or was this Terry guy just venting? Was he still in prison? If she could work up enough courage, she would read the remaining letters. *There is no might about it! I have to!* She needed to find some answers.

Picking up the packet, she stuffed it in the bag that David liked to tease her about. "It looks like you're leaving home," he'd joke. Pulling on her coat, she was determined to find out Terry's last name. Once she knew, she'd go to the library and check out the old newspapers they kept on film. If the crime he'd committed was serious enough to land him in jail for two decades or more, there surely would have been news coverage. Given the fact that he was a classmate of Damon's, he had to have graduated from the local high school. It must have been front page news. But first, she had to know Terry's last name. She'd dig out Damon's class book as soon as she got home.

Going to Mike's office, she ducked her head inside to tell the men she was leaving. "So far the correspondence I've found has nothing to do with the business," she told them. "I'll see you tomorrow morning. Tomorrow night for sure," she added, looking at Tom. "If there's anything I can help you with, just give me a ring."

"Will do," Tom agreed, looking up from the invoices he was studying. He wasn't so busy that he couldn't stop to look at her as if she were an important person. He was terrific, and the fears tearing up her peace of mind fled momentarily.

"I'll walk you to the door," he said, jumping up. "I need the exercise to fine tune the brain." It was as good an excuse as any.

As he held the outside door open, her steps slowed. "When I think of how Damon died just outside this door, I have to force myself to walk through it."

It was on the tip of her tongue to tell him about the letters, but she changed her mind just as quickly. Tom was a stranger, no matter how nice he was. Why should he be burdened with her worries?

"I thought something like that was troubling you." He laid an arm across her shoulders. The gesture wasn't one that suggested familiarity or possessiveness, but one that conveyed a feeling of caring. "Be careful out there," he cautioned, quoting a popular expression.

Once in her car, she wondered why the police hadn't looked through Damon's file. Perhaps because the building hadn't been broken into, neither had the offices or the plant, and so the files hadn't been rifled. Still, it seemed like negligence. Or, giving them the benefit of the doubt, a major oversight.

Chapter Six

THE SEARCH

Where should she begin looking for Damon's class book? That thought preoccupied her on the drive home and as she entered the house. She had unconsciously prided herself in believing she knew exactly where every single item was stored, either on shelves, in cabinets, closets, wherever. Now she was in a tizzy, not knowing where to look first. Before she began the search, she must let Brassy out. Then she looked in Damon's den, which seemed like a plausible place.

The den had been Damon's private domain when he was alive. She'd not gone in there since his death. The library was *her* private space. There she managed the household accounts, and Damon rarely had reason to go there. She'd not gone into his den except to dust and run the vacuum. She prided herself on not being a snoop, a wife who behaved like a basset hound, sniffing out every detail of her husband's affairs. Damon had given her orders that Nora wasn't to be allowed in there, for whatever reason he had.

The den, which they never referred to as a study, wasn't a large room. Now as she entered, she saw it was as conservative as Damon in character. Besides a leather wingback chair, the only concession to comfort, there was a desk, a filing cabinet, and a relatively small built-in bookcase. The shelves were far from filled. She knew from the times she had dusted that the books pertained, for the most part, to furniture history, production, manufacturing, and design.

The one large window was bare except for blinds, which she abhorred. To her the room was as tasteless as pancakes without syrup. But as long as Damon had wanted it that way, she had let it be. In time she would place a plant beside the window, find a striped sofa, perhaps put up some drapes and a painting. She had her eyes on a woodsy one with animals like those that wandered through the yard in their search for food.

But now, where might she find the class book? A quick scan of the books, which stood in precision order like good soldiers on guard duty, revealed nothing out of context with the subject of furniture. Definitely no class book. She turned to the oak desk to search through the drawers when she was interrupted by the doorbell's ring. *Now, of all times, she didn't want to be disturbed.*

Mary was standing outside, her coat collar turned up against the wind. Liz remembered that she hadn't given her a key. Brassy sat beside Mary, thumping his bushy tail. "How thoughtless can a person get?" she apologized, dismayed by her oversight.

She'd just opened the door when she heard the phone ringing. It was David, wondering how she'd been, what she'd been doing, and what was new. He called often, but he'd not called on Sunday, a day he rarely missed.

When, out of Mary's earshot, she told him about taking Mary in, he asked the exact same questions as Cory. Once he was satisfied that Mary was no derelict out to take advantage of his widowed mother, he tried to sound happy that Liz wasn't alone.

"Will she be there at Thanksgiving?" he inquired. "I can check her out then."

Liz knew in her heart that although he teased about checking out Mary, he was serious. Mary would undergo a scrutiny worthy of the FBI. Liz decided against mentioning the letters from the mysterious Terry, thinking she didn't want him to worry when he should be studying. David hung up, not entirely happy with the news from home.

She and Mary exchanged brief happenings of their day and made their way to the kitchen for lunch. Liz had no appetite now and hoped Mary didn't expect anything spectacular. There was the old standby, yogurt. And she could throw together a salad. "We'll have something substantial for dinner," she informed Mary, failing to see Mary's face fall in disappointment. "Glasses for milk are in that cabinet with the glass doors," Liz pointed to a cabinet door.

"You should teach a class on proper diet. Educate girls how to eat," Mary remarked, agreeably, going along with the meager fare and hoping Liz might at least have cookies for dessert.

"Do you think so?" Liz replied, then surprised herself by adding "I need to find Damon's class book."

She hadn't intended to tell Mary about the letters she'd found that morning, but Mary had told her all about her visit to her grandmother. As they shared, it seemed only natural to confide her deepest concern.

"Letters?" Mary asked, thinking she'd missed a link in the conversation.

"I found threatening letters from a man named Terry. Damon mentioned him once, and I am wondering if he's the same Terry who graduated with Damon. He was a friend of Damon's in high school." Liz gave a condensed version of his letters.

"Maybe you should call the police. Or take the letters to them."

"I suppose." Liz stopped chopping long enough to give Mary an appreciative look. "I haven't been thinking straight. My mind is a jumble. I think I'll read the other letters first—if I can stand to read another of those horrible things—and then try and find Damon's class book. The police would need to know the man's last name."

"It's enough to give a person the creeps. Do you think he might be the man who killed your husband?"

"That's what I've been asking myself. I think God sent you to me, Mary."

"I think God saw both our needs and brought us together," Mary said. Tears glistened in her green eyes.

"You just gave me more words of wisdom. I forget that God is at work in our lives."

"It seems like the thing to do. Go to the police, I mean." Mary finished her glass of milk and wished she had a sweet roll and a soda pop. "I do appreciate that you took me in. I don't know what I would have done. Grandma was so relieved that I have a place to stay. Now she knows I'll be around." Dabbing at her eyes with a napkin, she volunteered to help Liz search the house.

"Could you find him in your class book? I mean, if you went to the same high school, wouldn't he be in it?" Mary hoped her suggestion wasn't too presumptuous.

"Damon was eight years my senior," Liz explained. "Too far ahead of me to know him then. I was still a child." She managed a lame joke.

They found Damon's class book on a shelf in his closet, beneath a neatly stacked pile of slacks he'd outgrown. "Don't throw them out. I'm going to lose weight," he'd declared adamantly. He never threw anything away.

"Maybe this man's picture won't be in the class book. Damon said Terry dropped out of school two weeks before they graduated," Liz worried aloud as she scanned the glossy pages.

"It would have been published by then," Mary guessed. Liz marveled at the girl's clear thinking, surely God-given. She noted the enlarged date on the cover of the book. A mental calculation told her it was published thirty years ago. That was a long time for a man to spend in prison, if he'd gone in right out of high school.

"How will we know which Terry to look for?" Mary asked, viewing the pictures. "There might be more than one."

"There are autographs by some of the pictures," Liz mused. "If I remember correctly, he signed his. Most high school graduates go around getting their friends to autograph their class books." They'd seated themselves on chairs with cross-stitched seats in the upstairs hallway. Liz was too excited to take the book downstairs. Her heart was racing. With luck, she'd find Terry's picture.

"It would be something if this guy's picture is in here. To think he might be the one who—"

Mary halted in mid-sentence. She was reluctant to speak the terrifying word, *murder,* again.

Liz wagged her head slowly in agreement. She turned the next page and slowly scanned the pictures. One picture with an autograph scrawled beside it captured her attention.

She lifted the book from her lap to have a closer look. "It's his handwriting!" Liz spoke in hushed tones. How lucky could she get?

"You're sure?"

"I'm positive. His handwriting looks the same, anyway." Scrutinizing the picture of the innocent-looking student made her wonder what had happened to fill him with such hate. "His last name is Thompkins. Terry Thompkins. Very poetic for a murderer," she observed. "Now I must read the other letters and call the sheriff."

The rest of the letters were as ominous as the others. The last one was written exactly six months ago. Terry had been very meticulous about noting the date. It was a subtle way, perhaps, of stressing his threats.

The last one warned: *You haven't come across. I'll see you when I get out. And it won't be as a buddy.*

Liz read the chilling message aloud. "Call the sheriff," Mary urged her, throwing down the magazine she'd begun leafing through.

Out on the road, Terry sat in a stolen black Honda, the motor running, watching the house from a safe distance. He'd pulled up in time to see Liz open the door for Mary. "So the daughter is home," he said to himself, a smile on his sallow complexion. "That makes it easier to deal with both of them," he muttered, making a mental note of what kind of car the girl drove. He needed to plan how he would get to them. Should he knock on the door and barge in? Or should he wait until they left the house and surprise them? Or break in and be there waiting when they came home sometime? Somehow he wasn't as crazy about doing away with them now. Damon wasn't alive to know he'd get revenge. Then he thought of all the wasted years he'd spent behind bars. Getting rid of Damon hadn't been enough.

Chapter Seven

MEETING WITH THE SHERIFF

At nine the next morning, Liz was running short of time. She'd made an appointment with the sheriff before she called Tom Kelley to tell him she'd be a no-show at the office. "I'm going to meet with the sheriff. I'll explain later. I can call June Davidson if you need help," she told him. "That way you'll get to meet her. She worked for Damon in the office. He seemed satisfied with her work."

"I'd like to meet her," Tom assured her. "I'm glad you're going to talk with the sheriff." He didn't pry as to why she was seeing the sheriff, which she appreciated. She hung up and called June.

"Sure, I can go in and help," June agreed. Pausing briefly, she added, "I heard a rumor that the new owner is in the area and that he's going to turn the plant into a casino." Now that Liz was no longer the boss's wife, she felt comfortable passing on a piece of gossip hot off the grapevine.

"Rumors! How do they get started?" Liz chuckled. It felt good to laugh.

"That's the news on the gossip channel. I've heard it from more than one person."

"The new owner, Tom Kelley, isn't going to change a thing. He plans to keep the business running as is. He plans to rehire all the employees. I think you'll like him."

"Really? You mean I don't need to look for a job? Wow! It's almost too good to be true."

June had never talked to Liz before, except when Liz made rare phone calls to Mr. Pass. Then she'd never felt at ease talking to the boss's wife. The conversations had been brief and to the point. Now Liz chatted like any woman talking to another female. She didn't seem the type to have been married to Damon Pass. He'd been a real nerd. Mrs. Pass seemed pleasant and someone who had all her ducks in a row. Labeling Mr. Pass a nerd, even to herself, when the poor man had died a dreadful death, was terribly mean. June felt sinful just thinking it.

"The newspaper is planning to put a story in today's paper," Liz said. "A reporter interviewed Mr. Kelley yesterday afternoon." She knew because Tom had called and thanked her for contacting the paper.

"I'll call and tell Mr. Kelley I'll be happy to help. I'm dying to meet him," June admitted honestly.

The sheriff's office wasn't as imposing as Liz imagined. One officer sat at his desk, another wandered around, opening and closing files. Another was rifling through his desk, obviously searching for something. It was nothing like the confusing, bustling scenes she'd seen the few times she'd watched detective shows on television.

Sheriff Dawson sat hunched over, his forearms resting on his desk, appearing indifferent as Liz told him about the letters. "I believe he was a classmate of Damon's," she explained, carefully removing the letters from the zippered pocket in her handbag. Her hands shook as she laid the letters and Damon's class book on his desk. Her voice sounded unlike her own, a sign of nerves. Talking about the murder would always be difficult. She worried about how the sheriff would react to the letters. Scoff if he wanted, but there they were, and not to be treated lightly as if they were the figment of a silly woman's imagination.

Meeting with the Sheriff

"You were wise to bring these here," Dawson said, plainly dumfounded by Liz's discovery. She should have brought this evidence in the minute she found them. They might prove crucial in cracking the case. But he wasn't about to lecture her. Timing was everything. Over two weeks had gone by since Pass was murdered.

"Do you think this man might be the—the guilty one?"

Dawson avoided a direct answer. "The crime lab will look these over, compare the signatures with those they have on file at the prison. They'll check for fingerprints too. We need to find out what prison he was in. That won't be hard to track down."

"I wonder if he is out of prison now?" Distraught, Liz's perfect posture stiffened. Her lips trembled as she spoke. "I have two children, you know, both away at college. Thankfully."

"We'll get right on this," he assured her, patting the documents lying beneath his hands. As a father, he understood her concern. Now she was on the verge of tears. In an attempt to lighten her mood, he complimented her, "You are a real sleuth, Mrs. Pass. We could use someone like you in the department."

Liz grinned. "Thank you. That sounds like a job I might be good at. I've been finding things for my family forever." She smiled, remembering all the misplaced homework, lost socks, and nondescript items she'd found for the kids and Damon. But she was in no mood for light conversation. "Please let me know what you find out," she said, locking eyes with Dawson.

Dawson assured her he would be in touch the minute he found out anything. He was anxious for her to leave. He planned to put in a call to the State Police Post as soon as she stepped out the door. What she'd brought in appeared to be cold hard evidence identifying Pass's killer.

Chapter Eight

DAVID IN LOVE

David called late that afternoon. "Mom, I met the girl I'm going to marry!" He fairly yelled the words. She held the phone away from her ear and didn't miss a word. Did he think she had suddenly grown deaf? David was not his normal calm self. He didn't ask how she was as he always did. It was silly, but her feelings were hurt.

Liz was stunned. *This isn't David, my beloved son. He's not this impulsive!* All kinds of questions ran through her mind. Experience had taught her, however, not to react too quickly and to swallow any negative response even when the kids seemed to be inviting trouble for themselves. David had always been levelheaded and seldom needed counseling. But choosing a mate was a totally different matter. Trying to sound casual and interested, she asked questions she believed were pertinent and not too prying. "Wow! Where did you meet her? Who is she? Is she a student?"

"I met her in a bar."

She couldn't believe her ears. "A bar? What were you doing in a bar?" Her cool came out of disguise. If she was being too nosy, so be it. David never frequented bars. Besides, he spurned drinking.

"Three of us guys went to the bar to sit and talk and see if we might get an opportunity to witness to somebody about faith."

"I suppose that would be a likely place to meet non-believers," she said, trying not to sound too sarcastic. "But what about this girl? What was she doing there?" She wondered if this girl—David hadn't told her the girl's name—was a local barfly, looking to get her clutches on a decent guy.

"There's not much to do on campus. She needed a break the same as us guys. She was there with her roommate, who goes there all the time. She said it wasn't the smartest thing to do."

"Sounds suspicious." Liz's voice rose. She didn't care. Her son's future—his faith—might be in jeopardy.

"She's been studying hard. Her roommate invited her to go out. Janice, that's her name, went with her. She was lonesome for her family too. She'd never been to a bar before. She was completely out of her orbit. One look at her and you can see she's not the type to be in a bar."

"Janice is a nice name." Liz spoke the first thing that popped into her head. "Being in a bar *is* asking for trouble."

David ignored her remark. "I wondered if it's okay if I bring Janice home at Thanksgiving."

"She doesn't have parents?" Could anyone blame her for wondering?

"Oh, sure, but they live in Iowa. It's too far, what with the four-day holiday." He paused. "Is that girl, Mary, still there?"

"Yes, she's here. I haven't talked to her about Thanksgiving. She may be going down to her parents." Her head spun, thinking of all the details she needed to work out. "Maybe they're coming up here to see Mary's grandma. They wouldn't stay here, I'm sure. Do you really know this girl? I mean, how can you be so sure about her?"

"She's a Christian, Mom. She's pretty. She's fun. We talked for hours last night."

"You're only a senior. After this year, you have seminary ahead of you. Are you still planning to be a minister?" *Stop drilling him,* she ordered herself.

"Of course, Mom. Nothing can change my mind about that. We're not talking about marriage. Not yet. I just want you to meet her. Okay? Is there room at the house for her, even with that girl there?"

"Yes, there's room—unless Jessie invites a friend. I guess I need to get busy and furnish that room downstairs. We also have that spare room that only needs drapes or curtains. I haven't decided yet."

It was decided. David would bring Janice home. Liz was both eager and leery about meeting her. She hoped Janice was all David thought she was and that she wasn't a wimp, looking for a husband. David said Janice was pretty. Was she tall, short, slender, blond, brunette, dishwater blond, or a red head? Those things weren't important. David claimed she was a Christian. That was good. And she was in college. Another plus.

Her thoughts jumped to Thanksgiving. There were tons of things to do before then. Rolls and more pies to bake, turkey to buy and put in the freezer. The Lenox china that she used only for special occasions needed washing. The sterling polished. The linen damask tablecloth touched up with the iron. She wanted something clever for a centerpiece too. What a relief it was to think about something pleasant—if it weren't for worrying about David's new girlfriend. He'd dated a few girls, but after a time they were history. For David to be so smitten, this girl must be in a class all her own.

Liz had Tom Kelley's visit the next evening to think about too. Tomorrow she'd bake cookies. Everybody raved about her cookies, even though they were the standard, old-time favorites common to housewives: peanut butter, chocolate chip, oatmeal raisin. *Are you hoping to impress him? Of course not! It would be impolite not to have something to serve.*

The purpose of Mr. Kelley's—Tom's—visit was to meet Mary. How he happened to be coming here was a queer quirk of ungovernable circumstances. Or was it? Mary could just as well have gone to the plant. It was too late now to change plans. Better to leave things as they were. He might think she didn't want him to come here. What a silly woman she was to get herself into such a predicament.

Just handle it, she lectured herself. *Relax and be yourself. After all, it's not a date. But I want to look good. What should I wear?* She felt comfortable in jeans. Wearing them would make a statement. She wasn't viewing his coming here as a date. It wasn't a date, she reminded herself again. He was coming to interview Mary.

Chapter Nine

Man in the House

The next evening she kept imagining she heard Tom driving in. She ran to the front entrance and peeked out the window adjacent to the door two or three times to see if he was driving in. He'd said eight o'clock. She checked the time on the grandfather clock, an heirloom handed down in her family for several generations. It was a few minutes before eight. She could depend on the old clock. It was as accurate as Old Father Time. Then, without warning, the reflection of headlights flickered through the white pines, as if playing hide and seek, sending shivers of surprise down her spine. She shot a glance at her reflection in the hallway mirror, checking her appearance one last time.

She watched until Tom parked his SUV. Then without pretense, she swung wide the door. "Come in. It's cold out there," she urged him, feeling like a schoolgirl on her first date.

Brassy barked his customary greeting. *I feel like barking. But how perfectly silly you are to be so smitten by a near stranger.*

The spontaneity of her greeting warmed Tom's heart, if not his feet and hands. "I forgot how cold it gets here in the north," he said, removing his leather gloves and rubbing his hands together. Glancing around, he was impressed. "What a beautiful home, and what a perfect setting for a log house," he said. His look of admiration was for her as well as for the house. Few women in their forties—and she had to be in her forties—looked as good in jeans.

"Thank you." Liz blushed. *He complimented the house, not you, silly woman.* "Mary's in the family room," she hastened to add. "This way." Smiling, she indicated with a wave of her hand that he should follow her. Brassy scampered ahead.

She had built a fire in the fireplace, and for the first time she appreciated the ambiance of the room. Mary was seated on the plaid sofa perusing a magazine, her legs crossed, her free leg swinging up and down. She was nervous. Her good manners never lost a beat, however. She stood as they entered.

Liz introduced them. They chatted about the weather and how wonderful and relaxing it was to watch the fire. Liz seized a lull in the conversation to excuse herself. "I'm going to the kitchen. You two can talk."

"Oh, you don't need to leave," Tom assured her, jumping up.

"You know me, Liz," Mary interjected, sensing electricity between the two. "I'm not going to tell him anything that you don't already know."

"I have some refreshments in the kitchen," she rushed to explain. "What would you care to drink? Coffee, tea, a glass of wine, hot chocolate? Tom? I know Mary prefers Coke." She excused herself, happy to flee from her own bewildered state.

"Coffee sounds good, Liz," Tom answered, sitting down again.

Performing the simple task of arranging cookies on a festive tray calmed her. Tom was here being kind to Mary. How wonderful it was to hear their voices in the background, to have people in the house. Her eyes glistened with the mere pleasure of this blessing. Had she thought of it as a blessing before? No. She'd been blind to simple pleasures. It was as if she'd been blind, and now she could see.

When she entered the family room, Tom sprang up and stacked some magazines on the coffee table, making room for the plate of cookies she'd arranged so beautifully on the tray. She was impressed again by his thoughtfulness and self-confidence. He was quick to see what needed to be done and did it.

"It's all settled," Tom informed her as she took a chair on the opposite side of the fireplace. "Mary is going to be my gofer."

Puzzled, Liz's dark brows scrunched together until Tom went on to explain. "You know how every business needs somebody to run errands. To the post office. Or maybe go for a part for a machine. There will be any number of jobs she can do. Maybe help the girls in the office. Or Mike on payday. She says she has computer skills."

Mary beamed with excitement, a broad smile threatening to crack her lips. "I'll start next Monday," she told Liz.

Liz slapped her hands together in delight. "Perfect!"

"I think so." Mary lifted off her seat like a shot from a cannon. "Brad is going to call tonight. I can't wait to tell him the news." Snatching up two cookies, she was out of the room in a minute. This was the first time Liz had baked since she'd lived here. She'd treat herself, even if Liz gave her the eagle eye.

Liz thanked Tom, and their conversation eased into small talk. First, he complimented her on the delicious cookies. From talking about cookies, they moved on to the benefits of eating at home versus dining out. They both agreed that eating out at a fashionable restaurant was fun to do on occasion. They moved naturally to more personal subjects. Tom told her about how his wife had suffered, and that his marriage had been a happy one. Liz shared how Damon had already started the furniture business when she met him and how hard he worked to make it a success.

"Why did he decide to sell, if I may ask?" Tom wanted to know. For all the world, he resembled Paul Newman in his younger years. Not too tall, not too short. Nice shoulders, slender hips, dark hair.

"I really don't know. He was so private about everything he did. He didn't confide in me. I guess I wouldn't have had much to offer as far as the business." Lost for an explanation, she lifted her shoulders, a gesture defining her confusion.

"How unfortunate for both of you," Tom said, not intending to sound critical. He couldn't imagine any man not wanting to include this beautiful woman in every facet of his life.

Liz stared into the fire. Then she turned to him. She'd made a decision to confide in him. "I found threatening letters in Damon's personal file from a man named Terry. I took them to the police. He might be the one who...uh...murdered Damon."

Tom leaned forward, his elbows resting on his knees. His dark eyes were fixed on Liz's face, imagining the fright she must be feeling. "I knew you were upset about something when you left the office yesterday. Now I understand why. Have the police got back with you to report anything?"

"No, not yet."

"Do you think Damon wanted to sell because of the threats?"

"I haven't the faintest idea. Could be. That thought has been in the back of my mind."

"Keep me informed, will you, if the police connect this guy with your husband's murder?" He searched her face before adding, "I'm glad you have Mary here with you."

"She is a comfort, in more ways than one. She's a good kid. I like her. She's good company, and it feels good to do something for somebody." For the moment she forgot about the man named Terry. "I've made a commitment to the Lord to help girls in need of a home."

"That's a worthy thing to do. I admire you for it."

"I decided to take Mary in when the pastor preached about making a commitment. You may remember when he preached about having purpose in our lives. I feel this is my calling. I have this big house, and what good is it unless it's used for some worthy purpose? All I did was rattle around in it, feeling useless."

Liz listened to what she was saying and was amazed. These very thoughts had been gathering in the back of her mind but now were out in the open. Now that she'd given voice to her thoughts, they became tangible. Her commitment was a reality. Talking to Tom had acted as the cement that gave her commitment a confirmation.

"That's neat, Liz. I remember the pastor preaching about commitment. I saw you in church that Sunday. Remember?"

"Yes." How could she forget? She'd wondered whether or not he was married.

The grandfather clock bonged eleven o'clock, interrupting a companionable interlude. "I didn't intend on staying so long," Tom apologized, jumping to his feet.

"I've enjoyed it," Liz assured him. "I'm glad for Mary that you're willing to give her a job."

"Call me if you need anything. Anything at all," he repeated.

She took his full-length wool coat from the closet and handed it to him. He stood with it for a long moment, his eyes holding hers. "Thank you for a wonderful evening."

"Thank you." She felt the heat spreading into her face. She wished she could fall through the floor. But no, she didn't wish that. She loved being in his company. It was embarrassing, though, to blush all the time, her pleasure and embarrassment betraying her.

"I will be praying this mystery gets solved," he added. His words had the effect of a caress.

"Thank you," she murmured again, wishing she could think of something more sophisticated to say.

It seemed natural to embrace. Tom wrapped her in his arms for a brief moment. Liz responded by giving him a firm, quick hug. When she stepped back, she felt as if her legs were rubber.

He slid on his coat, with a departing smile, before pulling the door shut behind himself.

Liz leaned against the door, dizzy with swirling emotions. *Did I feel like this when I dated Damon?* She'd been crazy about him. Now she guessed, with the benefit of hindsight, she'd been in need of love. She'd wanted someone to love and be loved by. That was natural and acceptable. Like many young people, she'd been self-seeking without being aware of it. Youthful hormones had been a part of it too. Now she looked at Tom and saw beyond the handsome exterior. She saw his character. He was considerate, pleasant to be with, warm, and caring. He had personality plus, too, which she attributed to his faith. Not all Christians were so vibrant, but Tom exhibited all the attributes that made faith attractive to others. In her youth she'd not seen being a Christian as a "must be." She'd never given it a thought. Now, if she was totally honest with herself, even with the benefit of age, she knew she was as vulnerable as any woman would be to someone as vibrant as Tom.

Yes, there was no denying her feelings. Getting to know Tom and anticipating a growing relationship thrilled and delighted her. She might be older, but age had better equipped her with a sense of appreciation for anyone honest enough to give and receive love.

How wrong it was to think this way when Damon was barely in his grave! Her sin smacked her dead center in the heart. Or was it sinful? Going to church on Sunday morning hadn't helped her with any answers. Bible study seemed to be an answer.

Tom drove from Liz's drive with warm, tingling feelings. He needed to ask her if her name was Elizabeth. Elizabeth seemed a more appropriate name for such an elegant woman.

At the end of the drive, he saw a car parked on the other side of the road. At first he thought someone might be stuck, or having engine trouble. But the car was parked beyond the snow bank that had been shoved there by a road grader.

The driver took off, spinning his wheels, causing the car to careen from one side of the road to the other. The exhaust rising behind had a smoke screen effect. Tom guessed the occupants might be young people, necking. There were few houses on this road. The secluded spot would be perfect for kids to park and spark.

Following the late model Buick, however, he could make out only one person, probably a man. Apparently the driver had little or no experience driving on snow-covered roads, or he wouldn't drive at such reckless speeds.

Then, remembering what Liz had told him about the letters from the man in prison, he began imagining the worst. He reached for his cell phone and was about to call 911. But the Buick was speeding down the road, nearly out of sight. There hadn't been time to get the license number, even if he'd been able to see it. He'd call and report the incident as soon as he could get to a phone. It seemed to him that the police should be watching Liz's house.

Chapter Ten

CONVERSATIONS

Tom tossed and turned, unable to sleep after being at Liz's. Seeing the strange car on the road drove him crazy with worry. When he thought about how the driver sped away, it aroused his suspicions. The next morning while visiting with his sister over a breakfast of oatmeal, juice, and coffee—Maggie insisted on feeding him "wholesome breakfasts"—he told her that he was worried sick about Liz's safety.

"I'm going to call the police," he confided, sprinkling his oatmeal with brown sugar.

"You really are concerned about this lady," Maggie observed, refilling his coffee cup from the carafe squatting on the table. "I'm sure you've prayed about the situation."

"Yes, I am, and yes, I have." He gave her hand an affectionate pat. "I'd be concerned about anyone in her situation. Her husband murdered. The letters." He became defensive.

"I know you would be," she quickly agreed. But knowing her brother, she saw that he acted more alive and interested in life than he had since the death of his wife three years before. It was unfortunate that they'd never had children, who would have been a comfort to him. Now this lady had caught his eye, and her woman's intuition told her Tom was more than a little interested in this lady, Liz.

Tom scraped the last of his oatmeal from his bowl, then excused himself. "I'm going to call the police again. I didn't get any satisfaction last night from the man on duty."

"Why don't you stop on your way to work and talk to the police?" Tom had never minded some sisterly advice.

"Maggie, what would I do without you? That's the thing to do."

"Flattery will get you nowhere," she said, giving him a playful punch in the ribs. "I'll let you hang out here because you are my brother. No other reason."

Sheriff Dawson was standing in his office and had just hung up the phone. "What can I do for you?" he asked, easing his bulk into the swivel chair behind his desk.

"I'm Tom Kelley, new owner of Northern Products," Tom introduced himself and extended a hand. He never liked trying to impress people with his position. He got a bad taste in his mouth when anybody thought they needed credentials to get his attention. However, from experience and from knowing people, he knew status was the perfect credential to get a busy person's attention.

"Glad to meet you," the sheriff said, standing and giving Tom's hand a firm shake.

"I'll make this brief," Tom began, glancing at his watch, letting the sheriff know he wasn't going to take up a lot of his time. He was busy too.

"Good enough." The sheriff sat down and waved a hand, indicating that Tom should take a chair across from him.

"I've become acquainted with Elizabeth Pass, Damon Pass's wife. I'm sure you know who she is. I was out to her house last evening. She told me about the letters she found. When I was leaving her home, I saw a car parked in the road in front of her house. It seemed suspicious to me."

The Sheriff leaned forward, one hand resting on his knee, the other on his desk, plainly interested now. "What kind of car was it? Did you get the license number?"

"It was a green Buick. I think a 2003. But I couldn't get the license number."

"There have been three cars reported stolen in the area in the past two weeks. This guy, Terry Thompkins, is out of prison. We've confirmed that, and we are looking for him. He could be the guy stealing the cars. I'll check with the state police to see if they've had any reported stolen from around here the last day or so. The guy certainly couldn't afford one."

"Are the state police involved? Does this character have any family living around here?" Tom spouted questions as they came to mind until Dawson leaned back in his chair, subtly indicating that the interview needed to end. But Tom pressed on. "Liz, I mean Mrs. Pass, says he graduated with her husband. He must have parents or relations. Somebody."

"We believe he lived with foster parents. That connection is under investigation. We know now that the Terry Thompkins in prison was a classmate of Damon Pass. He hasn't reported to his parole officer, so he's already in big trouble, even if he is innocent in Pass's murder."

The sheriff started shuffling papers on his desk. Tom guessed he'd got as much info as he was going to get. He stood. "Let me know if you learn anything that affects Mrs. Pass," he added, speaking like a man accustomed to authority.

"Thanks for your interest," Dawson replied, ignoring Tom's request. "I've heard reports that the employees are relieved that they can have their jobs back."

"The news has circulated," Tom said, "in the newspaper and on the grapevine."

"That's our most active publication." Dawson's lips stretched into a smile.

Tom thought of a question he had to ask, whether it was any of his business or not. "Have you told Mrs. Pass that the man who wrote the letters is the same person who graduated with her husband?"

"Not yet. I was about to call her when you came in."

"It will frighten her. But she needs to know. She needs to watch her back." Tom wanted that impressed on the sheriff's mind, in case he hadn't thought of it already.

Dawson nodded in agreement. Did the man think he was derelict in his duty? Aloud, he said, "It doesn't seem that this guy would have any reason to hold a grudge against Mrs. Pass. But he was mad enough to kill her husband, and he's a threat to society in general. I am going to let her know that she was right in making the connection between the graduate and the guy who wrote the letters. She's a smart cookie!"

Tom left, feeling more burdened than before for Liz's safety. Prayer was the only comfort he had, and the only resource. Seated in his SUV, he bowed his head and prayed that God would watch over her, and that she would be careful and stay alert. "And Lord, guide the police in finding Terry Thompkins." Then, remembering Jesus' love and forgiveness for people, he added, "I know you love this man, and I pray for his salvation."

Chapter Eleven

WARNINGS

It was shortly after nine when sheriff Dawson called. Mary had just left to sit with her grandmother for the day. Liz was busy tiding up the kitchen. She'd set bread to rise for Thanksgiving. As Cory said, she already had enough for a small army, but it kept her busy. She was going to freeze all of it rather than tempting Mary by serving it for dinner. Mary had gleefully announced that she'd lost a whole pound.

Liz didn't recognize the sheriff's voice. She froze in place, fear clutching her in a frosty grip as bone chilling as the October wind howling outside. Was it Terry Thompkins? The more she thought about him, the more horrors she imagined.

"This is Sheriff Dawson," he said.

She plunked down on a stool, relieved.

"We found out that the prisoner who wrote the letters is the same one who graduated with your husband," he said, not wasting his time or hers.

"You are positive? You know for sure?" So now they were on the trail of the murderer, but it didn't lesson her fear. It merely put a face on Damon's murderer, if he *was* the murderer.

"They are one and the same," Dawson replied.

"Do you think I should stay here? What about my kids? They aren't here now, but they come home on breaks. Thanksgiving isn't that far off."

"Don't know," he hedged. "You could go away. If you stay home, keep your doors locked. Don't let anybody in that you don't know. If anything suspicious happens, call me right away. As of today, a patrol car will be cruising by your house every fifteen minutes."

Her hands were shaking when she hung up the phone. For the first time in her life, she got down on her knees, clasped her hands together, and prayed specifically. She prayed for the safety of the kids, for herself, and for Mary. "If that's not scared religion!" she chided herself. But she knew God understood and was available, waiting for people to go to him with their burdens.

Recalling that she'd read in Sunday's bulletin that a new Bible study was beginning at church, she began searching for it. On a hunch she looked through the stack of newspapers she'd put in the garage for recycling. Sure enough, she found it between sections of Sunday's paper. She called Mrs. Green, the woman leading the study, before she changed her mind.

"Wonderful! We'll be so glad to have you join us. It's this evening at seven o'clock. And please call me Betty."

Hanging up, Liz punched down the rising bread, happy to have something to take out her frustrations on. While the bread was rising, she decided to make a quick trip into town to pick up a few things she needed at the grocery store.

She'd just turned out of her driveway when she passed a patrol car. "That's a fast answer to prayer," she thought. Another car parked just past her house whizzed off, spinning his wheels on the slippery road. Evidently the driver had seen the patrol car in his rear view mirror. The police car gave chase. "That's one sure way to get a policeman's attention," she said to herself.

She was a mile down the road before she began to put two and two together. The driver could be Terry Thompkins. He'd seen the police and raced off. She hated living in fear like this, viewing every car and every phone call with suspicion. *Calm down*, she counseled herself. Thompkins had settled his score, whatever it was, with Damon. Why would he want to harm her? Or the kids for that matter? But then, he had threatened them in his letters. Who knew how a murderer thought? Her life was being controlled by fear. It wasn't fair.

She'd call Sheriff Dawson about seeing this suspicious car. On second thought, there was no need to. The policeman in the patrol car would report the incident. Maybe even catch the guy. Wouldn't that be a great answer to her heartfelt prayer?

She wondered why she hadn't thought to ask Dawson what Thompkins was in jail for. Sometimes she didn't think fast enough. Damon must have been as guilty as Thompkins, or at least Thompkins judged him guilty. Knowing what crime Thompkins had committed would solve that mystery.

The mundane chore of shopping was a pleasant diversion, one she rather enjoyed. She wheeled into a parking space, happy to put fear and worry behind. Once inside, she started down the third aisle, list in hand, looking for raisins and coconut. Then the "mad woman" as she privately referred to her, appeared in her peripheral vision.

Liz hoped to avoid her. She had no wish to engage in another verbal free-for-all with other shoppers as witnesses. She did catch a glimpse of the newspaper the woman had thrown in the seat designed for children. Half of Tom's picture stared out from the folded front page. The paper had capitalized on the story of the new owner and what it meant to the community.

Liz picked up her pace, but she wasn't fast enough. The woman's voice intercepted her.

"Mrs. Pass, why didn't you tell me the employees wouldn't be out of work?" She jabbed viciously at the newspaper with a smoke-stained finger, pointing at Tom's picture.

"Because I didn't know," Liz said, speaking in as civil a tone as she could manage. Several scorching retorts came to mind. The woman hadn't said she was sorry about Damon's death, or offered any apology either. But what did she expect from the reprobate? Her appearance was as pathetic as her attitude. Her coat looked as if it had never seen a hangar. Her hair was as greasy as the inside of a can of shortening, and her boots flapped open.

The woman's appearance was wretched, her attitude even more pathetic. Jesus had taught that you should forgive those who despitefully use you. *The "you" means her, Liz Pass.* Well she'd forgive her, but it was useless to stand and argue with her. "You don't believe me when I tell you the truth. I do hope you meet up with the truth and recognize Him."

The woman looked puzzled, then sneered, "Just give me one reason why I should trust you?"

"The truth lies in God's Son, Jesus."

"Don't spout religion. You think it makes you better than me."

"No, I don't. The only thing that makes me better inside is faith."

"I believe in God."

"Most people do. But they don't know Him. That's the difference."

"I didn't know you were a preacher," the woman sneered.

"I'm not. I'm a believer." Liz walked away, hurriedly picking up the items on her list that she remembered and forgetting the items she most needed: flour and baking powder.

The phone was ringing as she entered the house. Dropping the bag of groceries on the cabinet, she rushed to answer it. It was Cory, not Tom as she had hoped. "I haven't heard from you, Girl. What have you been up to?" Cory demanded.

"The usual. It's so good to hear your voice."

"All you need to do is pick up the phone and call me. Or stop by."

"I have lots to tell you. Can you come over? I have bread ready for the oven."

"Not more bread! Are you going into business? I'll drop over if you give me a loaf."

"You're terrible. But if I must bribe you, I'll give you a loaf."

They talked non-stop once Cory flew in the house—as if racing against time.

The top story for Liz was her fright regarding Terry Thompkins.

"Liz, I'm frightened for you. That murderer running around, and you living out here in the sticks."

"Mary is here with me."

"Mary! What good is she? She's gone a lot of the time."

The phone rang, interrupting them. Cory caught Liz's hand before she could lift the receiver. "Don't say anything until you know who it is," she cautioned.

Liz recognized Tom's voice. "Liz, are you there? Are you all right?"

"Hi, Tom. My friend is here, lecturing me about answering the phone."

"That's an excellent idea," Tom agreed. "I was wondering if the sheriff called you."

"Yes, he did. So now I know who, but I don't know why."

"Would you like to go out to dinner tonight?" he asked.

"I'd love to. But I committed myself to going to a Bible study at seven." She wished she had a legitimate excuse for not going. But she sure wouldn't tell the women she had a date.

"I'm glad you're going, but I'm disappointed. We can make it another night. I'll call you when you get home tonight. If I may?" She loved the way he was so polite.

"I should be home by eight-thirty. Nine at the very latest." Now she had his call to look forward to, which made up for her disappointment.

"You need to get caller ID," Cory said when Liz hung up. Then reverting back to her bantering mode, she asked, "Who's the guy on the phone?"

"He's the one who bought the plant. Remember, I pointed him out in church."

"It sounds like you've got something going." Cory raised her eyebrows and looked down her nose at Liz, giving her an eagle eye.

"I feel guilty about enjoying a man's company when it's been such a short time since Damon's death."

"You're not talking about marriage, are you?"

"Of course not! Don't be ridiculous." Liz's voice dripped indignation. "I have more respect for Damon's memory than that. There's nothing wrong with being friends with him, is there?" There were times when Cory could really raise her dander.

"Hey, you're a grown woman. Relax! Of course there's nothing wrong with being friends. But I heard recently that men and women can't be just friends. Sex is a natural development." She stopped lecturing when Liz glowered at her.

"That wouldn't be true of Christians." Liz was adamant.

"Oh, Liz, stop living in fantasy land. Christians are tempted like anybody else. And too many succumb to it."

"Cory, I'm not a child. But I do appreciate your concern. What would I do without you?" Liz leaned over and hugged her friend. "I know you love me, or I wouldn't put up with you."

She never needed to doubt what Cory was thinking. She was as upfront as anybody could possibly be. With Cory, what you saw was what you got.

"Well, I need to be shoving off," Cory said, glancing at her watch. "Stay in touch and don't forget this old friend." She lifted a hand, her thumb pointing back at herself. Leaning down, she patted Brassy, who scrambled from beneath her feet, barely avoiding being stepped on. "You guard her. Hear?" Brassy responded with one swing of his tail.

Going out the door, she said over her shoulder, "There's Gus plowing again."

"I like having him around when Mary's not here and I'm alone."

"That's good. Talk to you later," Cory dashed to her silver Toyota.

Chapter Twelve

GROWING COMMITMENT

At six forty-five that evening, as she was leaving to attend the Bible study, Liz was turning out her driveway when she met a patrol car. The police were watching her house. *Does it make me any safer?* Sheriff Dawson had called late that afternoon to tell her that Terry Thompkins' picture was going to be broadcast on television.

"Would it help if I put up money for a reward?" Liz asked.

Dawson hesitated. He knew the Passes were wealthy, but he had no idea how wealthy. Any reward offered would need to be a sizeable amount. "I'm sure it would," he answered.

"Is ten thousand enough?"

"That should do it." Dawson swallowed. "But it's best not to advertise who's paying the reward. Some screwball might believe you'd pay big money if one of your family was kidnapped."

"Don't worry," Liz snorted. "I don't want anybody knowing I'm offering the reward."

When she reached the church, she was tempted to turn around and go home. *My ignorance of the Bible will embarrass me to tears.*

These women will know chapter and verse, she rationalized, swinging her Buick Riviera into a parking space. Well she'd committed herself, and she'd see it through. If she didn't, she'd need to make some excuse if that Mrs. Green asked why she was a no-show. She knew from experience, unfortunately, that telling white lies set traps for larger ones. Telling the truth skewered the pride, but being caught in a lie was more painful. There was no turning back.

Entering the church, she hadn't the vaguest idea where the women met until she heard feminine voices coming from down the hall leading off from the sanctuary. *Why did I get myself in this predicament?* She could still get away without being found out.

She needn't have fretted. The women quickly picked up the telltale signs betraying her uneasiness. Her posture was like that of a manikin—rigid, unbending, and very subject to breakage. She clutched her Coach™ leather handbag as if it were a raft in raging water.

The women did everything but stand on their heads to put her at ease. They introduced themselves, asked if she preferred coffee or tea, and inquired about David and Jessie.

Later, summing up the evening, Liz had embarrassed herself in a most unlikely way.

She'd worn her navy wool pantsuit and red silk shirt, which was a major mistake. The other women wore jeans and sweatshirts or sweaters. She stood out like an orange in an apple barrel.

She hadn't thought to take her Bible, a dreadful oversight. Color crept up her neck and into her cheeks when Mrs. Green happily told her, "You've come at a perfect time. We're just starting a new study, the Book of Galatians." The women promptly opened their very own personal Bibles to Galatians. Liz had only a vague idea where to find Galatians. Was it in the Old or New Testament? Mrs. Green located a Bible and handed it to her, neatly turned to page nine-hundred and thirty-one. "This is the NIV translation," she told her.

Liz's insides tightened as if tied in sailors' knots when Mrs. Woods, the pastor's wife, smoothed the pages of her Bible with confident hands and began. "Galatians is so rich in doctrine."

What do I know about doctrine? Absolutely nothing. She knew her face was red as her blouse. She squirmed in her chair and stared at the open Bible on her lap.

"Doctrine is simply applying Christian attitudes to one's life, and acting on them. It's walking in the Spirit of Christ." Mrs. Green hesitated. "We'll see this application as we study."

Turning her full attention on Liz, she beamed like a spotlight on target. "If you don't mind Mrs. Pass, I'll use the way you took in Mary Hartley as an illustration. That was a wonderful way of showing Christ's love to another person."

"I've benefited as much as Mary has." Liz was embarrassed and attempted to counter the compliment. She didn't feel worthy of such praise.

"It required some adjustments on your part, I'm sure," Mrs. Woods insisted.

"I couldn't be that flexible," another woman admitted. Two or three others nodded their heads in agreement.

"If you have room, I know of two girls, fourteen-year old twins, who need a place to live temporarily," a Mrs. Soul piped up.

"I do have the room," Liz acknowledged. For the first time, the size of her house was a plus rather than an embarrassment.

"They were abused by their father," Mrs. Soul went on to report. "Their mother has signed off all parental rights. Their aunt took them in until their grandparents finish building on a room for them. The aunt has a family and is cramped for space. The situation was never reported to social services. The father took off somewhere. He knows he's headed for jail if he dares come near them. It's a sad situation." Mrs. Soul finished, removing her glasses and dabbing at tears clouding her eyes.

The pros and cons of taking in the two girls swirled through Liz's head. Her heart ached for them, but did she dare take them into her house with Terry Thompkins lurking around? On the other hand, the police were watching her house. When she stopped and thought about it, perhaps she was worrying unnecessarily about him bringing harm to herself or anybody else in the house.

If she did take them in, she'd need to buy beds and linens for the unfinished room in the basement, in case they were still there at Thanksgiving time. Thanksgiving was beginning to burgeon with people. The basement bedroom was finished except for furniture, and there was an adjoining bathroom. They'd be comfortable there.

"I have two college kids coming home for Thanksgiving," she said aloud, wondering how David and Jessie would react. The long weekend was a break for them, a time to relax and enjoy themselves. But knowing them, they'd be off socializing with friends. Or Jessie would shop, and David would be eager to show Janice around.

"I'll take them," she agreed. *Well, I've done it again. I've made a snap decision without giving it serious thought.*

"It will mean more giving of yourself and your time," Mrs. Woods warned.

"I'm sure." Liz nodded. She felt good about her growing commitment. She was doing something worthwhile for others. Her huge house was being put to use for a good purpose. For the first time in her life, she felt at peace with herself. She felt like celebrating. If she were a child, she'd buy a hundred balloons and set them free, one by one, to fly wherever the wind took them. It would be a small expression of how at peace she felt. The inner restlessness that had tormented her sense of well-being had flown away like birds flying south for the winter.

Chapter Thirteen

THE SUSPECT

In a small town thirty miles away, Terry Thompkins scraped and rinsed dishes, getting them ready to go into the dishwasher at the Wayside Family Restaurant. The manager had needed help "right now" and hired Terry on the spot, even though he had no social security card or any other credentials to identify himself.

"I'll bring all that stuff tomorrow," Terry lied, a manufactured smile pasted on his sallow face. He needed cash to survive. Working here he'd get an evening meal out of the deal, even if it were just a hamburger, which was fine by him. He loved restaurant hamburgers, couldn't get enough of them. They were something he'd craved while in the joint.

He had no intention of returning the next day. Staying too long in one place wasn't smart. He'd told the manager he'd just arrived in town, and he'd like his pay for the day so he could afford a motel room. "I stayed at a friend's last night and left my billfold there." It was easy to lie. People were so gullible.

The manager scowled unhappily, but he needed a dishwasher. "Okay. So your name is Delbert Lepien?" Terry nodded, acknowledging his new alias. He'd put the names of two prisoners together and come up with that handle.

The restaurant had a television turned on all day in the dining room. Terry couldn't see the picture from where he stood at the sink in the kitchen. He wished he could. Watching television was a luxury. But when the six o'clock news came on, he picked up some remarks made by the waitresses that grabbed his attention. "Ten grand! Wow!" one whooped. "That is, if it turns out to be the right guy! They aren't going to hand it to just anybody."

"I wouldn't want to meet up with him. Anybody who would murder somebody, point blank like that, must be totally wacky," the bleached blond broad declared.

"He's not a bad looking guy, but his eyes look kind of scary. He looks sort of familiar."

"You're kidding? Do you think you've seen him somewhere?"

"I can't place him right now. Maybe it will come to me."

"He's probably not using his own name. What was it? Terry Thompkins?"

Terry fumbled a plate, and it nearly slipped out of his hands. How had the police figured out he killed Damon? There was no way they could have found fingerprints, was there? He wanted the end of this shift to come so he could get out of here—fast! That dumb broad might finger him.

He'd done everything he could to change his appearance. He'd let his graying hair grow to the point where it dragged on his collar, and he'd dyed it a dark auburn color. The manager had insisted that he tie it back with a rubber band. He'd grown a beard too, and wished it would grow faster. It had grown long enough to disguise his prominent jaw. In the joint more than one inmate had asked him if he wanted his jaw rearranged. It would improve his looks, they taunted, looking to start a fight. Now all he wanted to do was scram out of here!

"Del," one of the girls teased him, "you trying to make us look bad? The way you're working, the boss will give you one of our jobs."

"Sure!" he retorted without looking up, trying to sound sarcastic. He kept working, even faster now. Thinking. Hoping he could get out of there without someone identifying him. What would he do if one of them fingered him? He checked the wall clock to see how much time was left before he could leave.

Now, since the cops suspected him, he'd need to be extra careful. Maybe he should forget about doing in Damon's old lady and kids. Twice he'd met cops going by Damon's house. Each time he'd been driving a different stolen car. Up until now he'd guessed it was a mere coincidence. Now that he knew they'd fingered him, he needed to be more cautious. He sure didn't want to pull another hitch in the slammer, or worse—the rest of his life!

He'd gotten satisfaction out of surprising Damon and hearing him beg for his life. He had to say one thing for Damon, he hadn't begged as much as he bargained. He'd tried to buy him off by offering a few thousand bucks, but it was too late. He'd warned him in the notes he'd written from prison.

"You know where you can put your money. Nothing can repay me for spending thirty years in the joint," he'd spat out, his thick lips twisting until they looked like pretzels. He got a thrill each time he remembered how he'd let Damon hope for a few minutes and then said, "No deal," and pulled the trigger. The look of surprise on Damon's face had been gratifying, tickled him pink—a platitude his foster mother had often used. The only thing was, the thrill faded and he had felt sick to his stomach. Damon had once been his friend. If only Damon had written him, or visited him. He must have been afraid of being connected to the racket they'd hatched as kids.

He should do away with Nora, too. She'd professed to love him like a son until he got into trouble with the law. Then he became a discard. She'd never visited him or written him one lousy letter, not once in all those years. How two-faced could anyone be? So much for motherly love.

He smiled to himself as he put plates in the dishwasher. He liked that name, Del. He'd go by that name from now on, or until he had to change it again. If only he could begin life over as easily as it had been to change his name. But there was no use trying to fool himself. No matter what he called himself, he'd still be Terry Thompkins, a man without family or friend.

Chapter Fourteen

THE GREATEST GIFT

True to his word, Tom called shortly after Liz returned home from Bible study. "You got home safely," he stated the obvious. "I worry about you driving around by yourself at night."

"I'm cautious, but I do get a little uptight, wondering where that lunatic is," she admitted.

"How was the Bible study?" He was interested in everything she did and loved the sound of her voice.

"I've got a lot to learn. The women were nice. You know, pleasant. And there was a surprising development."

"I know it's late, but if you don't mind, I'll drop over and you can tell me about it in person."

Tom was amazed at his audacity—inviting himself to her house at this hour. What was he thinking? He was behaving like a befuddled kid, experiencing first love. But there wasn't a doubt in his mind: Liz turned him on. He liked everything about her. He was charmed by her.

He admired her spunk, for one thing. Life had dealt her a hard blow, but she was carrying on, facing the challenge of living without a husband's care, taking charge of her affairs—financial and otherwise. She wasn't letting fear hold her captive. What was most important, she was seeking to know God better. These qualities were wrapped up in a charming package, personality-wise, and in a shapely body. The way she blushed was amazing for a woman her age too. Were those pink cheeks an indication of how she felt about him?

Liz's heart picked up speed. It pulsed like a yo-yo, rising and falling in her breast. "Yes, come over. I'm not busy." The laundry waiting in the hamper and the spills in the frig could wait.

In her excitement she'd forgotten about Mary. She remembered now that Mary hadn't greeted her when she came in. She was about to call upstairs until she spotted the note propped up against the single, tall jasmine-scented candle on the hall table. Mary had gone to see her grandmother. *A nurse called and said I'd better come back. Grandma's vitals are erratic,* Mary had scribbled.

What should I do? Liz asked herself. *Pray for Mary, yes.* That was most important. Then she needed to make a fast change into something more comfortable before Tom showed up.

Hurrying to her bedroom and into the bathroom, Brassy at her heels, she splashed her face with water. She needed that little refreshment. Then, slipping out of the navy slack suit and red blouse, she pulled on jeans and a purple turtleneck sweater. *I'm glad jeans are acceptable any place now. This is what I should have worn to the Bible study.* But that was history. She sighed. Worrying herself about it now wouldn't change a thing. She'd know better next time.

She was paging through the phone book in the library to find Tom's sister's phone number when the doorbell rang. Tom was here already! He must have broken all the speed limits, she guessed, delighted at the thought of him racing to see her.

She swung open the door and grinned. Something about his stance reminded her of a kid on a first date. "Come in before you freeze." She waved a hand like she might at one of the kids.

Tom stepped in, returning her smile. Happiness at seeing Liz made him as agile as a man many years his junior. Taking her hands in his as she reached for his coat, he leaned forward to brush her cheek with a light kiss. Color rushed up her neck and into her face. "I hope my impulsiveness isn't keeping you from something you wanted to do," he apologized, peering down at her and not appearing to be the least apologetic.

"I'm happy you feel free to—to come over." She had nearly said "to see me." To cover her confusion, she hastened to tell him about Mary's grandmother. "Come into the family room," she said, wishing to spend a few minutes with him. "Her grandmother has taken a turn for the worse, it seems."

"Oh, I'm sorry to hear that. I know Mary's been expecting this. Were you going over to the nursing home?" He followed her into the family room. With no fire in the fireplace, the huge room seemed cool and impersonal.

"Yes, the poor girl has no family here. Nobody to support her. You know the situation. She hasn't been living here long enough to develop any close friendships. So there's no one to care enough to sit with her. She needs me. But we can talk a few minutes. How are things going for you?"

"I'm searching for another place to buy lumber. I have a couple of places in mind," he said, taking a seat squarely in the middle of the sofa, a subtle invitation for her to take a seat beside him. Shyly she sat on the farthest edge of the end cushion, her body turned to face him.

"Elizabeth," he began, his elbows resting on his knees, "I can't play innocent. I think about you all the time. I know that it's too soon after Damon's death, but I think you're wonderful."

"I think about you, too." She met his gaze with eyes alight, glowing with happiness. She liked the fact that he called her "Elizabeth." "It is too soon," she said, casting around for the right words. "I can't deny it. But I'm glad you care about me. I guess hearts can't tell time."

"I do care, very much. You are so right. Hearts can't tell time." He kept his eyes focused on her. "I worry about you. I saw Thompkins' picture on the news. Now he'll know the police have discovered his identity. That should be enough to keep him away from here."

He didn't mention the reward, even though he suspected it would come from her.

"I try not to dwell on his lurking around here," she spoke quietly. The thought of Damon's killer bursting through her door and gunning her down was something she tried not to dwell on.

"Thanks for telling me how you feel about me." He sighed and leaned back against the cushion. "I suppose we must behave like adults and go slow in our relationship. Show respect for Damon's memory." He reached for her hands and took them in his.

"Tom," she murmured, turning to face him. He kissed her hair and then forcing himself to keep his emotions in check, passed a hand under her chin and over her lips. If he were to be trusted, he must practice what he had just said. But he longed for the time when they would be free to be open about their feelings, to bask in the luxury of loving one another.

"Liz, I'll drive you to the nursing home," he said, taking charge.

"But I might be there for hours, maybe the rest of the night, Tom."

"No matter." He dismissed her objection.

Once they were in Tom's SUV and on their way to Tender Care Nursing Facility, Tom asked Liz about the Bible study. "You said something happened that you are excited about."

"We talked about commitment. One thing led to another," she began. "There was a woman there, Jeanette, who said she knew of twin girls who needed a place to stay temporarily. They are living with their aunt, who barely has room enough for her family, until they can go to live with their grandparents. To make a long story short, I said they can live with me until their grandparents can accommodate them." She watched Tom's profile, curious to see his reaction.

"You are one brave lady." He took his eyes off the road long enough to give her an admiring look. "It's one thing to care about people, but quite another to put it into practice. Those girls might have all kinds of emotional problems."

"I'm sure. They have been abused. I don't know how. But I feel good about doing this. I have more than enough room. And I've always felt a void in my life. Now it's gone. Jesus wants us to have purpose beyond ourselves. I've found it."

"Yes, and I admire you. You are a generous, beautiful person inside and out. I like you even more for this commitment."

Liz opened her bag and searched around in all her personal paraphernalia until she found a tissue. "I wondered what you'd think," she said, giving him a radiant smile.

"Where will you put them?" Tom wondered aloud.

"There's a finished bedroom downstairs with a private bath. There's one upstairs too. But it would be more private for them downstairs. I need furniture and linens. That's about all."

"If you need a way to haul furniture, let me know," he volunteered. "If you buy furniture out of town, it will be expensive to have it delivered. Maggie said the local store doesn't have much to offer."

"Thanks, Tom. Maggie's right. I might do just that."

Mary was sitting in the corridor outside her grandmother's room. She was alerted to Liz and Tom's approach by the tapping sound of their footsteps on the hard, clinically clean surface of the hallway. Their faces glowed like two-hundred-watt light bulbs on a dark night. One of Liz's hands rested in the crook of Tom's elbow.

"How is your grandmother?" Liz asked, leaning down to give Mary a hug.

"I'm going back in her room after the nurse gets done checking her blood pressure, and whatever else she's doing in there. I had to get out of the room for a few minutes," Mary said, weeping silent tears.

"I'm so sorry, Mary. I'm going to stay with you." Seating herself next to Mary, Liz wrapped an arm around her shoulders.

"I'm so glad you came." Mary spoke in hushed tones. "It's hard to see Grandma fading away. But she is a Christian. She keeps saying she's ready to move into a mansion."

"That's wonderful, Mary!" Tom exclaimed. "We can pray that the Lord takes her quickly."

After an hour had passed, Liz urged Tom to go home. "You have work tomorrow. I'll ride home with Mary."

After making Liz promise to call if she needed anything, Tom left. As he strode down the hall, attempting to walk as quietly as possible, Liz's heart followed after him.

He was everything, and more, that she could hope for in a man. Surely Mary's need had given her more opportunity to see that Tom was a man who would encourage her in her faith. The scripture the pastor had read in Sunday's sermon returned to her now.

"Love is the greatest gift of all gifts." Scripture made no exceptions. Of course, the author was referring to God's love, but men, being created in God's image, were capable of giving that gift, emulating it. Liz hugged this thought to her heart, believing that surely love is the greatest gift anyone could give or receive.

Chapter Fifteen

THE PAST UNCOVERED

Mary's grandmother died a few days later. Mary had slipped in to sit with her at ten that morning and was sick at heart to see her sweet old grandma struggling for breath. "I can't breath," she gasped. Being hooked up to oxygen wasn't helping. She'd been suffering a chronic pulmonary disorder that hadn't responded to treatment.

"I'll call the doctor," the nurse assured her, rushing out the door. Five minutes later she appeared with a syringe in hand. "This will help her relax," she reported to Mary, briskly administering the medication the doctor had prescribed. Within fifteen minutes, Grandma Fuller had passed on to a better world.

Mary's parents arrived in Middleton to make arrangements for the funeral. They chose the local funeral home Liz had employed for Damon's funeral. It was demoralizing for Liz to go there for visitation. Fortunately, Mary's grandmother's memorial service was held at the Methodist church she had attended before entering the nursing home. Liz was relieved. At least the setting wouldn't conjure up raw memories of Jessie sobbing her heart out, doubling her own grief. Nothing wrenched her heart as much as when she saw one of her children suffering emotional pain.

Mary's parents stayed at a motel, but Liz was worn out by the time the funeral was over. She made dinner for them one evening and sat with them at the funeral home during visitation. That involvement, plus adjusting to being a widow, taxed her energy. And…always lurking at the edge of her thoughts was the worry of Terry Thompkins. Where was he?

Somehow she'd found time to purchase solid oak twin beds, matching chests of drawers, bedding, and bath linens. As she shopped for the furniture, she saw a chaise that in her mind's eye she could imagine sitting in her own bedroom. She'd always wanted one. Without another thought, she told the saleswoman to add it to her bill.

"It was on sale," she told Cory, feeling guilty for spending money on something that was a luxury. When she and Damon were first married, they'd had to watch how they spent every penny. Those hard times had conditioned her to spend money cautiously.

Another chunk of emotional time went to Mary, who debated whether to go back to Detroit and live with her parents. "Are you sure you want me to stay?" she queried Liz, searching her face for any sign of wavering.

"You have a job here. And you're welcome," Liz assured her, giving her a hug.

"But you have the two girls coming to live with you."

"They won't be staying for more than a few weeks," Liz assured her. And so it was settled.

Then another front page story in the newspaper had rattled her nerves, keeping her awake the night it crowded out Iraqi war news.

According to the report, Thompkins had worked one day at a restaurant. His disguise had prevented the owner and the employees from recognizing him. When he didn't show up for work the second day, the manager wondered why. Thompkins had said he needed money, and he'd insisted on being paid at the end of the day. When he didn't return, the owner of the restaurant became suspicious. He knew his suspicions should have been aroused when the man claimed he had forgotten his billfold.

Seeing his picture a second time on television, one of the waitresses said she thought the mysterious employee was Thompkins. The state police had been called to check for fingerprints. They found one on the dishwasher. It matched up with Thompkins.

"He's getting desperate," the anchorman on the eleven o'clock nightly news reported. "He may be armed and dangerous. Contact the police at once if you see him."

On the morning of the funeral Nora arrived, red-eyed and looking frazzled. It wasn't her scheduled day to clean. Liz had just finished dressing and was digging bread out of the freezer for the lunch following the funeral when Nora banged on the door and barged in, surprising Liz. Nora was never this forward.

"Mrs. Pass," Nora insisted on calling her Mrs. Pass, or Missy, "I have something to tell you. You will hate me when you hear it." She began to sob and reached into the pocket of her worn black coat for a handkerchief bordered with tatted lace. "I can't work for you anymore."

"Why? What are you talking about, Nora?" She'd come to think of Nora as a friend. What could possibly have happened to give Nora such a ridiculous idea?

"It's so terrible," Nora sobbed, her head wagging back and forth in dismay.

"Come, sit down and tell me," Liz said, guiding her to a kitchen chair. Gently, even though Nora resisted, she slid her coat off and placed it over the back of the chair and motioned for Nora to sit down. She poured two mugs of leftover breakfast coffee and sat down beside the distraught woman. The funeral was scheduled to begin in an hour. If Nora weren't in such a state, she would tell her she needed to leave in a few minutes.

"You've done so much for me." Nora rocked back and forth in the chair. With shaking hands she lifted her cup and sipped at her coffee. Then, gathering courage from Liz's urging, she began spilling out her tragic story. "I think I told you once that I was a foster mother. That was a long time ago."

Liz nodded. For the life of her, she couldn't imagine how Nora's being a foster parent would keep her from working for her. What was she getting at?

Fresh tears pooled beneath Nora's eyes and overflowed. "I had a boy who was like a son. I loved that boy. I couldn't have children." The cup in her hand shook. "Early this morning the police came to talk to me." She stole a furtive look at Liz. "He is Terry Thompkins, the one the police believe killed your husband. That's why I can't work for you anymore." She covered her face with her tear soaked handkerchief.

The clock ticked off the seconds above their heads. Words failed Liz. She sat, staring, absorbing what Nora had told her. Laying a hand on Nora's, she spoke the only words of comfort that came to her. "You're not to blame for what he did," she said. She put herself in Nora's place, feeling her pain.

"Terry lived with me and Will for eight years. We tried to teach him right from wrong. But he got into trouble and went to jail. Will was so angry and embarrassed. Our names were in the paper and everything. Will didn't want anything to do with him after that. He didn't want me to write Terry. I did a few times, but he never wrote back." Tears splashed into the coffee cup trembling in her hand.

"What did he go to prison for?" It seemed a logical question.

"He was peddling hard drugs, I guess. You know—cocaine, heroin, weed. When an undercover agent tried to arrest him, he stabbed him. It didn't kill him. Just wounded him.

Lucky for Terry, or he would have got life. Another kid was with him, but he got away."

Liz's head spun. She guessed the rest. Damon had been the other kid. She was certain she wasn't jumping to conclusions. Damon and Terry had been dealing drugs, and Damon's only penalty had been a guilty conscience. If he suffered from guilt.

Now she remembered how often Damon had lectured David and Jessie about getting mixed up with the wrong crowd; how many times he'd warned them that using drugs was asking for trouble. Yes, those had been his exact words. "Drugs only lead to big trouble." Apparently he had learned the hard way. She wondered

The Past Uncovered

now if Damon had used drugs, or if he only sold them, which in a way was far worse.

Knowing Damon and his love of money, she guessed that his chief motive for selling drugs was for making money. How chilling to think that what he'd done had ruined lives, all because of greed. Had he felt any remorse? Was it from drug money that he had finances to start the business?

One thing was certain. The mystery was solved. She knew why Terry Thompkins hated Damon. He hadn't been caught and locked up in prison as Terry had. She prayed the children would never learn of their father's past.

She debated whether she should tell Nora about Damon and Terry's relationship. It seemed that since Damon and Terry had been friends, Nora would remember Damon. If she didn't, Damon certainly remembered her. She supposed that was why Damon had objected to Liz's hiring her.

"Damon and Terry were friends in school," Liz said, her voice just above a whisper.

"Terry didn't bring his friends home. Maybe he was ashamed of us. We lived in a small house. The same one I live in now."

"I see," Liz mused, grasping the pathetic facts.

"Terry held grudges. He must have held one against your husband all these years." Nora began crying again, mopping her eyes with her saturated handkerchief.

Liz pulled some tissues from the counter and handed them to Nora. "What Terry did has nothing to do with you, or with your working for me. You are my friend. You're innocent. I want you to work here as long as you want, but…," Liz paused briefly, "I think it would be wise to call the police and tell them about your relationship with Terry."

"They already know. But how did you know Damon and Terry were friends?" Nora asked.

"Damon, I think, was the other kid. I found letters Terry wrote Damon while he was in prison," Liz blurted. She covered her eyes with her hands and sobbed. It was too much. Anger twisted her heart and then her face. Oh, she knew she had been a bystander in Damon's life, standing on the outside, looking in. He hadn't trusted her enough to tell her his past, of his foolish, unbelievable mistakes. He'd been too proud to admit he wasn't perfect.

Nora gaped at her, at a loss for words. She took Liz's hands in her worn ones. It was her turn to console this lady who was so dismayed by the cold hard facts of her husband's past.

"Nora, I'll say it again. You are my friend. I want you to work for me. Don't ever think otherwise."

"You are wonderful, Missy," Nora gushed, rising to pull on her coat. Once she was out the door, Liz rushed to repair her mascara, stuffed the loaves of bread in a carryall bag, and dashed out the door. A glance at her wristwatch told her she barely had time to make it to the funeral.

Learning of Damon's involvement with drugs left Liz feeling guilty about the wealth from Damon's travesty. Money she spent was tarnished by thoughts of where it originated. She'd always wondered how he'd managed to start a business as a young man. True, he'd worked hard and used his ingenuity, but drug money had surely financed the starting up of his business.

On the way home from the funeral she stopped at Cory's and told her about her conversation with Nora. She needed a listening ear, and Cory was always a good listener. Cory hugged her briefly, sympathetic with Liz's concern. It took her the space of a few moments to volunteer her advice. "That was years ago. Forget it. You aren't to blame for Damon's sin. Don't fret about something you can't change." Leave it to Cory to put things so succinctly.

"It still doesn't seem right," Liz worried.

"Donate a chunk to some charity. Maybe a rehabilitation center. Some place like that."

"I can do that," Liz agreed, doubting she'd ever be rid of the guilt feelings.

Chapter Sixteen

THE TWINS

The aunt's house where the twins were staying was a few blocks from where Liz and Damon had lived in the old neighborhood. She had no difficulty locating it. Neither did she find it hard to imagine the family had to be packed like sardines in the small house.

The girls' Aunt Margie opened the door, carrying a chubby baby girl on one hip. "I wish I had more room. I'd keep the girls," she explained after introducing herself. She and Liz stood in the cramped living room while the twins were collecting their things. "My parents will love having them," Margie confided. Switching the baby from one hip to the other, she paused. Lowering her voice, she whispered, "I am so angry with my sister. I could strangle her."

Liz understood anger and sympathized with Margie. While she pondered a response, Margie shielded one side of her mouth with her free hand. "You should know what's gone on with the girls," she warned.

"Perhaps," Liz agreed, realizing she should have asked about the girls' background before taking them on.

"I think you need to know," Margie repeated, rubbing the baby's back now. "The girls are acting out. If you know what I mean."

With a jerk of her head, she indicated that Liz should follow her. Marge led her into the kitchen, which was a housewife's nightmare. She made no excuse for the clutter of pots and pans, baby bottles, dishes in the sink, and a stained towel that appeared to have been used to wipe up coffee grounds. This woman could use a dishwasher, Liz thought. She wondered if the twins hadn't helped their aunt.

"Acting out?" Liz asked, puzzled. She'd never heard the expression.

"Yes, they are hurting bad. Their mother gave up her parental rights, signed them over to our parents. I understand why they are disturbed. What kid wouldn't be? They mope around and don't cooperate. You'll need to be firm. They need love and patience. I'm too busy to devote as much time to them as I'd like. Besides everything else, I drive them to school every day. My parents are hoping to adopt them, if their delinquent father shows up."

"Where's their father?"

"He's a drunk and a doper. He took off somewhere. We don't know where. Good riddance! He knocked them around. They left the house one night and came over here."

Liz stood dumbfounded. This was a view of the world she'd only evidenced on the evening news. It was scary to know she'd be dealing with some emotionally scarred children.

"I take it you never imagined that such things happened to innocent kids." Margie's voice turned critical. She'd seen the incredulity registering on Liz's face.

"Of course I know such things go on, but I've never known anybody personally who's experienced such abuse, if that's what you mean," Liz answered, feeling on the defensive. "How dreadful for the girls to feel unloved and unwanted."

"Thank God for my parents. They care enough to take them on at their age, retired and all."

Meeting the girls, she never would have guessed they were twins. Donna was at least an inch taller than Dana, who was not only shorter, but also more petite. Only in their facial features was there any resemblance. They might have been sisters with different birthdays, Liz mused. Then she felt them scrutinizing her, wondering, no doubt, if they could trust her, what kind of person she was.

The late autumn sun highlighted Dana's light brown hair, which was stringy and in need of a shampoo. The same was true of Donna's dark brown hair. *They aren't scratching so they must not have lice,* Liz decided, knowing she was judging them unfairly. Their eyes were the same identical blue.

Once the suitcases were in the trunk, Donna heaved a sigh of relief as they climbed in the back seat of Liz's Buick. Why, Liz could only guess. Was she relieved at leaving her aunt's?

Aunt Margie, with the baby in her arms, waved at them from the living room window. Watching the twins in the rearview mirror, Liz saw them return limp waves, their faces blank and void of any expressions. Were they sad or stoic or angry with their aunt?

"We're on our way," Liz said for lack of something better to say. There was no response from the back seat. Both girls stared at the back of her head. She unconsciously reached up and smoothed her hair.

"I used to live down that street," Liz told them, nodding towards a street they crossed.

"Are you married?" Dana asked.

"I was married. My husband died a month ago."

"What's your last name?" Donna asked.

"Pass."

"Your husband was murdered, wasn't he?"

Liz sucked in her breath. Donna was trying to intimidate her. "Yes, he was."

"So, aren't you afraid the killer might come after you?" This girl was bold.

"I certainly hope not." Glancing in the rearview mirror, she peered at Donna. "You must watch the news. Or read the papers."

"I can't believe my aunt let us come and live with you." It was a flat out challenge.

"She may not have known it. I don't believe you'll be in danger." Liz kept her voice as crisp as a dill pickle and just as spicy.

There were no further comments from the back seat until Liz turned into her long tree-lined drive. "Why are we stopping here?" Dana demanded.

"I live here. This is my house."

"You're kidding! Wow!"

Brassy met them at the front door, barking and sniffing. "Is this your dog?" Their response to Brassy was warm enough. They stooped down and reached out their hands to pet him. Brassy licked their hands and leaped up, licking their faces with welcoming doggy kisses. They giggled.

"I'll show you to your room. It's downstairs."

"You mean in the basement? Does our aunt know you're putting us in the basement? We don't rate a room upstairs?" Donna sneered. Dana made a face.

"I think you will like it," Liz assured them. "It's this way." She gave them no time to do any more griping. She walked down the hall and toward the polished oak steps leading downstairs, leaving them no choice but to follow.

She was glad now that Damon had insisted they finish the walkout basement. "Jessie and David can entertain their friends here. Why wouldn't they like it down here?" he'd asked, gazing around at the fireplace and French doors leading outside. Now, as they reached the bottom step, the fireplace gaped at them like a person without proper etiquette.

Liz led the twins into the hall off the recreation room and opened the door to the bedroom.

"This is your room." Liz stepped aside, allowing them to enter first. Light shone through the window on the south wall that was larger than any in their aunt's house.

"It's like being upstairs," Donna said, plainly in awe of the room. Her eyes widened as she took in the ruffled chintz spreads and shams. Looking down, her feet began exploring the floor. "There's even carpet!" Liz had heard the last of any sarcastic remarks.

"Your bath is in here." Liz stepped over and opened another door.

"This is better than I thought it would be," Dana crowed.

"Thank you," Liz said, pleased. "I furnished the room after I knew you girls would be staying here." If she expected any expressions of appreciation, none were forthcoming. Glancing at her watch, she told them it was time for lunch.

"Do we have to eat now?" Donna whined. "We ate whenever we wanted to at Aunt Margie's."

"It's a house rule. We'll eat together." Liz spoke firmly, offering them no other option. "You have time to unpack first." On that note she turned smartly, leaving the girls to their unpacking.

She supposed she should have asked them if they liked tuna sandwiches made with homemade bread. She'd soon find out. If not, she'd get out the peanut butter and jelly. She was hungry for bread. Being mindful of Mary's need to drop a few pounds, she'd purposely avoided serving any for dinner. Mary was working today, and she was free to indulge herself, at least for this once. She was approaching her forty-fifth birthday, and she was on guard lest she succumb to middle-age spread.

Chapter Seventeen

FEAR AND FAITH

The next morning as Liz stuck a fork in the chicken cooking on the stove to test whether or not it was done, her mind was busy with thoughts regarding the twins. What Donna had said about being in danger while they lived with her struck a nerve. Liz had dismissed Donna's question at the time, thinking she was a rude teenager, acting smart and attempting to have some kind of control over her sister's and her lives. If she could make Liz feel guilty and irresponsible, Liz's credibility would be undermined, not trustworthy. Not good. She had disregarded it, believing Donna was acting out her hurt and anger at her parents and everybody in general.

Now as she worked at the counter, preparing chicken salad for lunch, Donna's question played over and over in her head like a cracked forty-five record of her parents' era. What if she was compromising the girls' safety? The hands on the kitchen clock stood exactly at ten-o'clock. She'd give Aunt Margie a call and ask her what she thought about the girls staying with her. The twins and Mary were downstairs in the recreation room getting acquainted in front of a roaring fire. She could talk freely without being overheard.

Margie didn't sound thrilled when Liz announced herself. She was about to give the baby her morning bath, and there were the dozens of other things staring her in the face that needed her attention: folding laundry, dishes, vacuuming, the usual. She hated to admit it, but it had been such a relief to have the twins out of the house. The extra laundry and two more mouths to cook for had pushed her to her limits. They'd been so mouthy and unappreciative of everything she and Rob had done for them. She had to give Rob credit for not losing his cool. They had treated him so disrespectfully. He understood where they were coming from, he told her. Now she suspected Mrs. Pass had her fill of them already and wanted to send them back. She couldn't blame her. If that were the case, she'd call her parents and insist, "Take them now, ready or not."

Liz didn't know where to begin, and so she blurted, "Did you know my husband was murdered?"

"No, I didn't," Margie answered, wondering what that had to do with anything. Why was the woman digging up her dead husband, who'd probably been murdered eons ago?

"It happened a month ago," Liz said, choking up.

"Oh, I'm so sorry."

"He was the owner of Northern Products."

"Oh, I guess I did hear something about that."

Apparently her husband didn't work at the plant, Liz told herself, or she'd know. "Now the police are wondering, for good reason, if I might be danger."

Margie waited for Mrs. Pass to go on, bracing herself for the bad news. So far she hadn't been able to draw any conclusions from what Liz rambled on about.

Liz plunged on. "I'm concerned about the girls' safety while they are here. That's what I'm saying."

"Do you really think you are in danger? Or that they are in danger?"

Finally she's catching on, Liz thought. "I don't know for certain. The police are watching the house. I just wanted to tell you. While they are here, I'm responsible for them."

"I will call my parents and tell them. See what they think." Margie sighed, relieved that she could pass the problem on to her parents. One more thing to do. Of course, she wanted what was best for the twins' welfare. At the same time, she wondered if the woman's imagination was running away with her.

"You didn't report the father's abuse to social services or the police?" Liz prodded.

"They are aware of it. Yes. But as long as the girls were safe they didn't do anything about it. I told you my parents are hoping to adopt them. Anyway, the agencies are so busy with their backlog of cases, they haven't got to this one yet."

"You can understand my position. Like I said before, while they are here, I'm responsible for them."

"I'll call my parents and see what they want to do," Margie repeated. *Whew!* She felt guilty for thinking it, but it was a relief. Mrs. Pass wasn't hinting that she wanted to send the twins back.

Liz hung up feeling discouraged and not at all enlightened. Instead, she felt more like a child lost in a supermarket, not knowing what to do, or whom to turn to. Her mind whirled, imagining the worst-case scenarios: Thompkins killing her, injuring the twins, or frightening them out of their wits. *Get a hold of yourself. Calm down.* She forced herself to turn her thoughts in a more positive direction. She remembered how Pastor Woods and the women in the Bible study were constantly harping that Christians should pray about everything. She would pray.

Kneeling down beside a kitchen bar stool, she rested her head in her hands and prayed. She'd never prayed on her knees before. Even with jeans on, the tiled floor was hard and cold. "God," she prayed, "I've got myself in this situation, and I'm scared. I don't know what I should do. I don't know whether I've put these girls in danger or not. Who can I turn to?"

No answer came from the other end. She got up, feeling more discouraged than before. "Are you there, God, like they say you are?" Her words sounded hollow and pathetic in the stillness of the kitchen.

I can call Tom, she decided. Lifting the phone, finger poised over the buttons, she had second thoughts. This was Saturday; he might not be in. Or if he *were* at the plant, he would be busy getting things organized and running smoothly. She didn't want to be a pest, running to him with all her troubles. At this stage of their friendship, they hadn't reached a point in their relationship where she felt free to call him with every problem.

Her thoughts returned to Pastor Woods. He said repeatedly that he was there for anybody who wanted to talk. He knew her situation and that she'd taken in Mary and the twins. Her long fingers flew, punching in the church's number.

Suddenly, before the pastor answered, it was as if a light flashed on in her head, quieting her mind, clearing her thoughts. God had given her direction! It was intended for her to call the pastor. It was her end of the connection with God that was faulty.

"I understand what you're saying," Pastor Woods said in his clear radio announcer's voice. "I'm sure you're concerned. I wondered if you'd thought this thing through. Taking in teenagers is a responsibility, and worrying about their safety on top of everything else must be wearing you down. You can be sure God is in this with you. I'll tell you what. We have room at the parsonage. The girls can live with us if need be. Let me give this some thought." He paused as if thinking what was the best advice to offer. "You should have some legal protection, something stating that you are their legal guardian while they are at your house. I have a lawyer friend. I'll give him a call."

Liz hung up, slightly relieved. She was receiving some help. Outside the kitchen window, the sun broke out from behind a cloud. Her spirits lifted. How wonderful to see the sun! Next summer she had plans for the yard. She'd have flowers of every description.

She returned to busying herself with the salad. While she washed celery, sliced grapes, and chopped almonds, her mind was occupied with thoughts of her commitment.

When she committed herself to taking in girls who needed a place to live, it seemed like such a perfect thing to do. She had the space and monetary means and the desire to take on this commitment. Now everything had gone wrong! Her motives had been pure. Or had they? She stopped chopping to quiz herself. Perhaps she had made the commitment for her own purpose. She'd needed to get her mind off herself. She'd been so lonely in this cavernous house. Yes, she hated admitting it, but her own interests had been a prime motivation. What she had decided was a worthy cause, but there wasn't true heart involvement in her commitment. She was doing it more for selfish reasons than for anyone else.

"Forgive me, Lord," she prayed, leaning against the ceramic counter. The sun, beating in the window, warmed her, comforted her like an invisible blanket.

The words were no sooner out of her mouth than a mysterious, wonderful peace cradled her entire being, body, mind, and heart. Surely, God was with her. He'd heard and answered her prayer asking for forgiveness. He had been waiting for her to get her head on straight. The commitment of which she had been so proud hadn't been made with the purest intent. God wanted her to love Him above all else and to do everything for his honor and glory, not for hers. She needed to be mindful that God loved the twins. She had to remember that they were God's children entrusted into her care

"I'm a slow learner, Lord," she confessed, picking up her serrated knife.

The phone rang, slicing like a knife through her newfound peace. She wanted to clasp it to herself, cherish it, and she resented this interruption.

"Hey, girl, have you heard the news?" Cory was eager to give her the details of a recent news broadcast.

"No, what's going on now?"

"You'd better brace yourself. You won't believe it!"

"Well, tell me!"

"Terry Thompkins, the guy who…uh…uh…" Cory stammered, still shy about referring to Damon's death as murder.

"The man who shot Damon," Liz finished for her. "Have they caught him?"

"No such luck. They said on the news that he broke into Nora's house this morning. She was Terry Thompkins' foster mother. Did you know that?"

Liz, phone receiver in hand, collapsed on a kitchen stool. She hadn't told Cory about Nora's connection with Terry. "Yes, Nora told me a few days ago. Poor Nora. Is she all right?"

"She wasn't home. He ransacked her house. The police have been keeping surveillance on her house, but somehow he managed to get in without being seen."

"I suppose he knew the layout of the house," Liz guessed. Goosebumps broke out on her arms. If he could break into Nora's without getting caught, he might do the same here.

"He was after money, according to the news reporter. Nora's husband hid money around the house, and this devil knew it. After the husband died, she deposited their savings in a bank. So the reporter said. Smart woman."

"I'm so glad she wasn't home. Now I'm really scared."

"I knew you might be. It's better that you stay alert. Surely, he'd know you wouldn't be foolish enough to keep money in the house."

"Small comfort." She was being sarcastic. "If he broke in here, it wouldn't be for money. It would be for revenge." Merely thinking of the possibility gave her cold chills.

"Maybe you should move out until they catch this guy."

"Where would I move to? The pastor said the twins could live with them. But there's Mary. Jessie and David are coming home for Thanksgiving. I don't want the holiday ruined for them."

"It's better to be safe than sorry," Cory lectured. "You're welcome to stay with Ben and me, you know. You and the girls."

"I might consider it, but not with the twins and Mary. That would be too much." She paused, turning things over in her mind. "Thanksgiving is a week away. I feel confident that things will work out." Liz, remembering the peace she'd experienced before Cory's phone call, trusted that everything would work out, somehow, someway.

"I'll see you at church on Sunday, won't I?" Cory asked.

"Yes, I'll be there, of course. See you then."

Chapter Eighteen

LUNCHEON DISCUSSION

Liz picked at her food, forcing herself to eat. The girls would wonder why she wasn't eating. She'd spent a good share of the morning fixing the chicken salad which was one of her personal favorites, but now she had no appetite. She was worried about the safety of them all. The thought of poor Nora, walking into her house and finding it ransacked, worried her. How was she handling it? She saw no reason to tell the twins. They didn't know Nora or her connection with Damon's murderer. If she confided in Mary, she'd want to go over and help put things back, straighten up the mess. She'd call Nora after lunch. Christians weren't supposed to worry, but how could she help it?

"I want to take the girls to a movie tonight," Mary said, waiting for her approval, "unless you have other plans for them."

"That's fine with me, if the girls want to go. As long as it's a decent movie." The twins lit up like Christmas trees, then stared at her as if she had dropped in from outer space. A movie was a movie. When they were with their parents, they saw anything they wanted. They weren't innocents.

"*Narnia* is playing," Mary informed Liz.

"I've heard that is a good movie." Liz nodded her approval. They would be safe, away from the house. "Are you going to the seven o'clock show? Tomorrow is Sunday."

"What does it matter what day it is?" Donna asked. She hadn't washed her dark brown hair yet, and it looked two shades darker. One hand was poised over her plate, gripping her fork like a shovel. Liz fought back an urge to tell her how to properly hold the utensils. There was so much she could teach them.

"On Sunday I go to church. I want you girls to go with me." Selecting a plump grape from the salad with her fork, Liz nibbled it.

"Church! We never go to church. I'm not going." Dana's fork clattered on her plate where it bounced off, settling on the clean lunch cloth.

Mary was watching and listening to this scene, wondering how it would play out.

"While you're staying with me, I expect you to go." Liz spoke more firmly than she'd ever spoken to her own kids. Of course, Jessie and David had gone since they were able to walk. She'd brought them up expecting to go.

"Why do we need to go to church?" Donna pouted, challenging her.

"Sunday is the day to worship God."

"I don't believe in all that stuff." Dana leaned back in her chair, crossing her arms across her flat chest.

"How do you know what you believe if you've never gone to church?"

Right on! Good answer, Mary thought, helping herself to another serving of the salad..

"I've heard about church on television and from my mom. It sounds boring," Donna added, sneering at Liz as if she were an idiot. "It's for people who need a crutch."

Where had she heard that criticism before? Liz asked herself. The memory wasn't one of her fondest. How could the girls put any faith in what their mother told them?

"Your mother?" The words escaped before she could toss them into the trash bin of her subconscious.

Dana's face twisted; convulsive sobs wrenched her body. Embarrassed, she covered her face with her hands. "My mom. I want to see my mom!" Muffled as they were, Dana's words torched Liz's heart.

Liz sat for a long moment, riveted to her chair. Her heart wrenched her out of the chair. Going to Dana, she stooped down, leaned her cheek against Dana's, and whispered, "I am so sorry, Dana. I know you miss your mom." For a moment her eyes slid toward Donna. She was seated across the table, staring at her as if she were a criminal of the worst sort.

"I miss my mother!" Another explosion of words rose from the depths of Dana's wounded heart.

Automatically, Liz brought Dana's head to rest on her shoulder. With her free hand she smoothed her hair, the only way she knew to offer comfort. What to say? She hadn't the faintest. She couldn't imagine a mother divorcing herself from her children's lives. As for the twins, the thought that their own mother rejected them, that she didn't love them, would scar them for life. Oh, she'd like to give that mother a piece of her mind!

On the other hand, she needed to get herself off the judgment seat. Surely, their mother would one day regret how she'd abandoned them and suffer as they had suffered. One day she'd stand before God and be held accountable. She was another person to pray for.

In the meantime here she was, responsible for these girls' welfare—physically, emotionally, and spiritually. She'd made a snap judgment and taken on the responsibility of caring for them, not thinking about their total well-being. Now she silently prayed for the words to comfort Dana and Donna. They were in desperate need of hope and confidence in order to get on with their lives and to rise above their parents' failure to give them the love and environment that was their right.

"God created us to be His friends. If we reject Him and His Son, we miss out on the good things He wants to give us—like the ability to accept ourselves, to love other people more than ourselves. Without God in our lives, we get royally screwed up. That's why I want you to go to church and see if you don't want to choose to have God in your lives."

"So," she continued, "if you want to call God my crutch, He is. I admit that I need a crutch. God helps me in my daily life. You girls are here because I was lonely, and God pointed out what I could do about it. I have this big house, and instead of being lonely and miserable, I am sharing it."

Dana's sobs subsided into hiccups. Donna was looking down at her fists, clenched on each side of her plate. "Mom played a mean trick on us, and I hate her!"

Liz kept her silence. At that moment, to lecture that hate was wrong would be futile. She was sure the twins would despise her if she said one thing against their mother. Time and faith, if they found faith, were the only remedies for this wounding affliction.

"There are kids your age who go to Liz's church," Mary spoke up. "Maybe you know some of them."

"Do you go?" Donna turned blazing blue eyes on Mary.

"Yes," Mary answered simply, returning Donna's gaze with a smile.

"We don't have any dresses to wear." Dana spoke now, a glint of rebellion in her eyes. Surely, not having dresses to wear was a legitimate excuse.

"You may wear jeans," Liz interjected, "but it might be more acceptable if you wear something that covers your navel." With a grin, she added, "I don't see anything beautiful about navels."

"Navel! You call them navels?" The twins' faces twisted into smirks, looking at one another and smirking at Liz. The tension vanished for the moment at least, and the mood around the table lightened.

Liz joined in, willing to laugh at herself. "Well, what do you call them? I suppose you call them belly buttons?"

When the laughter subsided, she pressed the subject of what the girls could wear to church. "Jessie has some shirts like the girls wear now. We can look through her closet," she told them. The thought flashed through her mind that Jessie might not approve of their going through her closet, invading her privacy. She hadn't been wild about Jessie's choice of shirts, but they covered what should be covered.

Luncheon Discussion

What a morning, Liz mused as she and the girls cleared the table. Too much emotion. First the news of the break-in at Nora's, and now the awareness of just how deeply the abandonment of their mother had wounded the twins. She had planned to tell them that it might be necessary for them to live elsewhere, but she decided against it, for the moment anyway. She'd wait to hear from the pastor and to see what the lawyer had to say. Given their history, they might misunderstand and feel that she, along with their parents, considered them unwanted discards. If she decided she should leave, then they surely would understand.

Chapter Nineteen

PHONE CALL

Liz planned to read and relax that evening after the three girls left for the movie. She built a fire in the fireplace and settled in the wing chair beside it, Brassy at her feet. She picked up the book she'd purchased, the third in the *Mitford* series. The first two books had been delightful, exactly what she needed to take her mind of Terry Thompkins. She read a paragraph but found it impossible to concentrate. She read the same paragraph a second time. The quiet emptiness of the house and the haunting noises outside overpowered her ability to absorb what she read. An eerie feeling crept over her. She felt frozen in the chair, unable to move, as if any movement she made would attract some lurking evil. Was that noise someone walking on the deck? Brassy sensed her uneasiness and lifted his head, listening. Then, jumping up, he barked, terrifying her. Had he heard something outside?

Slowly she lowered the book and moved her hand toward the phone that rested on the end table and picked it up. What if the line had been cut? As she raised the receiver to her ear, the phone rang. Startled, she jumped and dropped it in her lap. Fumbling to pick it up with hands that acted as if disconnected from her brain, she waited, listening to see who was calling.

"Mrs. Pass, we will be in your area on Monday measuring homes for seamless gutters. We'd like to give you an estimate." She was relieved to hear a human voice belonging to some harmless individual who was merely trying to earn a living. She was irritated too. "I have gutters, thank you," she said and hung up.

She saw a space between the drapes where she hadn't drawn them tightly together. Anyone could see her through that crack if they were on the deck. She forced herself to get up and pull the cord. "I hate Terry Thompkins!" she said. Brassy wagged his tail in agreement.

The phone rang again. Another strange voice, a man's voice, sneered, "You're home this evening. Waiting for me to call, were you?"

He hadn't said he was Terry Thompkins, but she had no doubt it was he. She was so terrified that she was immobilized, unable to speak. Her jaws worked, but she couldn't speak. Suddenly outrage claimed her, casting fear aside. This man was evil incarnated! She wasn't about to give him the satisfaction of knowing she was a nervous wreck. What could she do or say that would change his calloused heart and mind? The murderous creep! Anger locked her hand around the receiver and pressed it against her head until her ear hurt. Heavy breathing hummed over the line that reminded her of a wounded animal in pain. Well, he was wounded, spiritually.

Her mind was spinning but not out of control now. Reason returned. Since Thompkins was calling her, then he couldn't be anywhere near her house. Obviously he didn't have a cell phone. He couldn't afford one. Of course, that couldn't be ruled out. There was the possibility that he had purchased one and risked being identified by a salesperson. There was also the possibility that he'd stolen a car with a cell phone in it. If that were the case, he could be right outside, watching the house.

You're being foolish, she counseled herself. Sheriff Dawson assured her that men were watching the house. Thompkins couldn't be close by. Unless he had walked through the woods and was out there where they couldn't see him. From what the sheriff had said, the police were watching from somewhere other than the road.

Phone Call

That was reassuring. She told herself that this man had been created by God and was loved by Him, the same as she. On the other hand, God gave everybody free will, and this man had chosen to be evil.

"What do you want, Terry?" She addressed him by his first name in as stern a tone as she could manage.

"That's sweet, calling me by my first name. How do you know who this is?"

"I didn't know. I guessed. I want you to know that I know why you killed Damon. But what have you got against me?"

"You're his wife. You must know why I went to prison. That makes you guilty too."

"I knew nothing about his involvement. You can believe that or not."

"I don't believe you. I just want you to know I hate you. You're as guilty as Damon."

"Hating uses a lot of energy. It's a big problem, Terry. I try not to hate you even though you have made my life miserable. But I forgive you, because God gives me that commandment."

"Now isn't that nice," he sneered. "You know what you can do with your forgiveness!"

Reasoning with the man was futile. She wasn't a criminal psychologist skilled in dealing with a hardened criminal. She hung up.

Terry's phone call had purged her of fear. It had also drained her emotionally and physically. She needed the sound of a friendly voice. She could call Cory, but why upset Cory this late in the evening? If she made any calls, it should be to the police.

Fumbling in the directory, she located the number for the police station. The officer on duty reassured her that the police were keeping a tight surveillance on her house. "We believe he's left the area," the police officer told her. "We've been told that he took a bus out of town after he held up a drugstore."

"You're positive of that?"

"We don't have any reports of a stolen car in town, but one was stolen fifty miles from here, down in Cedarville. The owner says he has a cell phone in the car. It's just a matter of time now before we catch this guy."

"I hope so!" Liz exclaimed emphatically.

She picked up her book. The warmth generated by the fire relaxed her. She was engrossed in the book and what was happening to Father Tim, when the phone rang again. She let it ring. She'd been foolish to answer it before. The answering machine would pick it up.

"Hello, Elizabeth. This is Tom. I was checking to see how you are. I heard on the news that Nora's house was broken into. Give me a call, and tell me you are all right."

She grabbed the phone and punched the button on the receiver before he hung up. "Tom! I'm here. I didn't answer until I knew who was calling."

"You're catching on. The telemarketers make it a habit to call in the evening."

"I know. I had one not long ago. I'd welcome one of those calls over the one I just had."

"Who called?"

"Terry Thompkins." Her voice caught. "I called the police right away."

"I'd like to get my hands on him. I suppose the girls don't answer the phone?"

"They weren't here. Mary took them to a movie."

"How would you like to go out for a cup of coffee? Or better still, I'd like you to meet my sister. She'll make us a cup of coffee. She's not doing anything."

Her spirits spiraled like a top set in motion. He wanted her to meet his sister. Tears of relief and joy suddenly rolled down her cheeks. "Sounds perfect!" she answered.

Chapter Twenty

EVENING TO REMEMBER

Tom was at her door twenty minutes later, giving her barely enough time to freshen up her face, change into a red flannel shirt, and run a comb through her hair. *I'm lucky to have been born with natural wavy hair,* she thought again, viewing the back of her head in a hand mirror. She didn't mind that nature was sprinkling white amongst the black, either. Coloring it would be a bother. Jessie told her she should color it and switch to a more mod cut. "I'm quite happy with it the way it is," she'd responded.

When she opened the door for Tom, the wind threatened to tear it from her hands, sheltered as it was by the porch roof. Snow flew in, pelting her with soft flakes that melted the moment they landed. Tom stood, his head hunched down inside the collar of his blazer. He'd hurried away without a coat or gloves.

"Tom, you're going to freeze!" Her maternal instincts took precedence over any warm greeting. "Come in," she urged, pulling him inside as she blocked Brassy from dashing outside.

"It's getting to be a blizzard out there," he said, stamping his feet and welcoming the rush of warm air from within the house. He rubbed his hands together, a trifle embarrassed for rushing out improperly dressed. In his excitement over seeing Liz, a coat and gloves had been furthest from his mind.

"You said the girls went to a movie," he said, stating what he already knew as fact. "I hope Mary knows how to drive in this weather."

"She's been driving on slippery roads since she came up here, but not in anything like tonight. I wouldn't have let them go if I'd known we were in for a blizzard. I didn't listen to the forecast for tonight. Now I'm worried about them."

Tom's presence made her feel young and alive. It seemed natural for him to be there, in her house. "Your sister is expecting us, but do you think we should stay in rather than hazard going out?" she asked. "It would mean more driving for you."

"My Explorer has four-wheel drive. But why put it to the test? You can meet her some other time."

"There's a fire in the family room. Go in and get warm while I make coffee," she said, settling the question. "Use the phone in there to call your sister. And the fire needs another log or two, if you don't mind."

After he'd tended the fire, Tom joined her in the kitchen. He had no intention of missing out on one minute of being in close proximity with Liz. He wanted to see her doing things, even the mundane things like measuring coffee. She had a natural grace about her that had to be innate. Women who were given to jealousy must envy her. *I wonder if she knows it?*

"I thought I'd join you." He sounded casual as he slid on a bar stool at the counter. Gazing around he admired the layout of the kitchen. "This is what could be labeled an ideal kitchen," he commented.

She pivoted neatly and nodded her head, a smile lighting her face.

"Do you like to dance?" he asked. His question was totally unrelated to what they'd been talking about, but she didn't ponder over an answer.

"I liked to dance as a girl. I used to dream of dancing with the Rockettes," she assured him honestly. "What made you ask?"

"I don't know why I asked." He passed a hand over his face, embarrassed. "You have a natural grace when you walk."

"Thank you, Tom." She was blushing again. "Damon didn't like to dance, and I didn't press him."

"I enjoy dancing. There must be a place where people can dine and dance."

"Sounds wonderful! I know there is." She sparkled at the suggestion. It was something to look forward to.

"We were talking about your kitchen." He chuckled at how off the wall his remark must have sounded.

"This kitchen is easy to work in. We hired a professional to design it. I specified that I wanted a country kitchen with plenty of light."

"You've got that. Speaking of kitchens reminds me, I saw Nora being interviewed on the six o'clock news. According to what they said, and from the televised pictures, Nora's house was torn up big time. It wasn't damaged, but things were dumped out of drawers, furniture shoved around, that kind of thing."

"I am so sorry for her," Liz stopped in the midst of removing cups from a shelf. "From what Cory heard on the news, Nora's husband never trusted banks. His parents lost money in the thirties, you know, in the Great Depression, and he picked up a mistrust of banks from them. He kept money hidden in different places around the house. Nora was smarter than that, thank the good Lord. When her husband died, she opened a savings account. Thompkins didn't know that, of course."

"According to news reports she did have bills on her dresser that Thompkins took," Tom added. "Not too much, I suppose, but more than she could afford, I'm sure."

"I'm so glad she wasn't home. He's wicked!"

"He must be desperate for money to risk getting caught."

"When I heard he'd broken in, I was worried more than a little bit. If he dared break into her house, he might break in here." Goosebumps broke out on her arms at the very thought. "It's enough to shake a person up."

With coffee in their hands, they moved back to the family room and seated themselves, one on each side of the fire. Just like old married couples, she thought. She smiled at Tom, wondering what he was thinking. He was seated on the edge of the chair, looking at her over the rim of his coffee cup. Lowering it, he returned her smile. "I'm glad there's a storm. I like being here with you."

Damon had rarely joined her by the fire. When he did, he ignored her for the most part. He read the newspaper or magazines of interest to him. It was unfair to Damon's memory, but she couldn't help but make comparisons. It was amazing how her ego got a lift from Tom's attention. Of late she'd become more confident in the knowledge that God had created her, that He intended her to be an individual. She had worth as a person. To have that reinforced by God's presence in a person was like a confirmation of the Spirit.

"How is it going at the plant?" she asked, attempting to make conversation and to appear calm and collected.

"I'm pleased with the way things are falling into place. I'm not fighting the union. The wages aren't unreasonable. Most of the employees have returned, and it wasn't difficult to replace those who didn't. There are lots of people looking for work. But tell me about the phone call," he said, rising and taking a seat on the floor beside her. He stretched his legs out, his feet crossed at his ankles. He looked up at her as he spoke.

"It gives me the creeps to think about it. I'd been sitting here alone, imagining I heard sounds outside. It's amazing how the imagination works over time when you're frightened. Then the phone rang, and it was him."

"What did he say?" Tom asked, waiting for her to continue.

"He thinks I'm as guilty as Damon. He wouldn't believe me when I said I didn't know a thing about Damon's involvement."

"You called the police?" He was too polite to ask what Damon's involvement had been.

"Yes, as soon as I hung up. They said he is fifty miles from here." She paused, looking into the fire. "Earlier I was thinking that I should take the girls and go somewhere, maybe to a motel. I was so stupid to bring them here. I put them at risk."

"You brought them here with the best of intentions," he said.

"The twins are so full of anger and hurt. I dread telling them that they must go somewhere else to live. I don't want them to think I'm abandoning them. But if Thompkins is on the run and headed south, maybe they *are* safe staying here. I don't know what to do." She put her head in her hands.

Tom got up and moved to the sofa. He patted the cushion beside him. "Come and sit beside me, wonderful lady."

"You are full of it." She smiled, unable to resist his invitation. The warmth of his body, as she took a seat beside him, was delightfully exciting and comforting.

He wanted to put his arms around her. Instead, he took her hands in his. Then, with her so close, the temptation was too much. He brushed her forehead with a kiss. "I'm sorry you're having all this worry."

"I know you are, and I appreciate it," she said, leaning her head on his shoulder.

An undeniable expression of love softened his face, which she was oblivious to. "Liz," he said, "about the twins. Do you have anything in writing, an official document, to protect you in case they get ill or hurt and need medical attention?"

She lifted her head to look at him. "I have been stupid. I did call the pastor. He said he'd get in touch with a lawyer who goes to our church. He'll get back with me as soon as he talks to him."

The phone rang, startling Liz. She jumped up, preparing to answer. At any other time, her reaction might have struck Tom as humorous.

"I'll answer it," Tom told her. She was only too happy to let him take charge.

Snapping up the phone he said, "Pass residence."

There was no response from the caller. "This is the Pass residence," he repeated.

"Mr. Kelley?" The voice was familiar.

"Mary?"

"Oh, Mr. Kelley, my car is gone. It's not where I parked it."

"Where are you now?" he asked, wondering who would steal that rust bucket.

"We're here at the theater."

"We'll be there as quick as we can," he assured her.

Liz was anxious and pale, expecting the worst.

"The girls are okay," he told her as he hung up. "Nothing to worry about except that they need a ride home. Mary's car was stolen. Can you believe it? Somebody was hard up for a car." He couldn't help but smile in disbelief.

Chapter Twenty One

THE LOVE OF CARS

Terry Thompkins stole cars for the simple reason that he liked driving them. He rarely had trouble stealing one. People were so stupid. They thought their cars were exempt from being stolen. They left keys in the ignition as if they were protected by some kind of invisible shield. One night he'd sneaked into a garage and found a car with the keys left in it. He'd crawled in the back seat and slept for a few hours and then took off before the owner found him. The dream that had kept him sane in prison was the thought of getting behind the wheel and driving again.

He'd driven old Will's car after he turned sixteen and got his driver's license. That was one good thing he could say about Nora and old Will. They'd let him use the car for school events, which he didn't always show up for. That's how he got in trouble, he had to admit. He'd run into drug dealers and started selling the stuff. Damon had been in on it with him. Things went along without a hitch until they met a dealer who turned out to be an undercover agent. Damon was inside the store, trying to buy some liquor. When the agent told Terry he was under arrest, he'd stuck him in the gut with the jack knife he kept in his pants pocket. Another agent popped up out of nowhere, and his life on the outside was history. He'd never squealed on Damon, his friend. *Friend! Ha!*

He'd thought Damon might hire a lawyer, help him out somehow. But the ingrate had never visited or written a note.

The morning after breaking into Nora's house, he knew he'd better scram out of town. He'd risked hitching a ride with a trucker headed south, contrary to reports that he'd taken a bus. The truck driver didn't care who he was. He wanted company on his long haul.

He hadn't been in a drugstore either, like news reporters said. That would have been crazy with surveillance cameras in stores, taking pictures of anybody who walked in. Of course, his beard had grown to a scraggly length, his clothes were dirty, and he smelled like an animal, so he might not be recognized. He hated being dirty and unkempt. He wanted to travel south and try to make a life for himself, establish a new identity. Mexico was looking better all the time, if he could get across the border.

He'd hitchhiked because he didn't want to spend money on bus fare, and there was more chance of being recognized. Once he was in Cedarville—the police had been right on that detail—he'd found an unlocked car, with keys thrown on the seat, outside a supermarket. He'd decided to back track then, since he'd heard on the car radio that the police were on the lookout for him, expecting him to be traveling south.

It was while heading north that he used the cell phone in the car and called Liz Pass. He had found Damon's number in the phone book the day before he shot him. He had a good laugh, remembering how scared Damon's old lady sounded, until he remembered her sounding off about religion. She forgave him because it was a commandment. *Give me a break!*

When he got back to Middleton, the old hometown, so called, he was on the outskirts of town and cruising past the theater. He recalled going there as a kid. His reverie was halted when he spotted Damon's kid turning into the parking lot. He remembered her beat up old car. It would be a neat trick to steal it, he decided on the spot. By the time he turned around and drove into the parking lot, he saw three girls making a mad dash from the car to the theater. Apparently the daughter had friends with her. All the better!

Their evening of fun was about to change. He parked the stolen car next to the daughter's. The kid's car was twelve years old, at least, and was a cinch to open and hotwire. Damon must have been a tightwad to let her drive such a wreck.

Once he was back out on the street, he thought about where he might spend the night without getting caught. He would freeze to death if he slept in the car on some back road in the woods. The weather was getting fierce now. The wind was blowing out of the north. To top everything off, it was snowing, becoming a blizzard. When he'd been in the pen, he forgot how Michigan weather could change as fast as a snap of the fingers. He remembered the saying, "Wait five minutes in Michigan and the weather will change."

As he drove, he thought about being in Nora's house that morning. It had seemed like going home. *Don't be such a sap!* He'd almost cried as he moved around the house. Memories threatened to turn him into a crybaby. He recognized the same furniture and doilies in the very same places they'd been thirty years ago. And not a speck of dust to write your name in.

It was the only home he remembered, having gone to live with Nora and Will when he was only a young kid. His parents had dumped him. He knew nothing about them except that they didn't want him in their lives. As he moved around Nora's, he'd snapped out of his mood when he remembered that she'd never written him one lousy letter, not a line.

Wouldn't it surprise her if he showed up on her doorstep? The idea appealed to him the way a hot plate of food would. He was so hungry, the thought of food made him drool. With the cops thinking he was south of here, they might have called off the watch they'd placed on her house. Without giving it further thought, he turned down the next street and headed for Nora's for the second time in twelve hours. It was less than two or three miles, on the other side of town.

The streets were snow-covered with an inch or more of the miserable stuff. It took him nearly an hour to get there. There were no tracks on either side of the street where cars parked, and very few had traveled down the center of the road. He decided to chance it. Parking the car two blocks away, he got out, bracing himself against the blizzard that threatened to send him spinning off balance.

At Nora's the drapes were pulled, blocking any chance of seeing who might be inside. He walked up the three steps leading to the porch, his shoes crunching in the snow. Boots weren't part of the issue when he was released from prison. He heard what he thought was a television playing inside, which surprised him. Will hadn't approved of television, said it was the devil's advocate, so he'd missed out on watching television like other kids except at Damon's house. Damon's parents were rich, and Damon got about anything he wanted.

He listened for voices other than Nora's and those from the television. Hesitating before he pressed the doorbell, he looked up and down the street and around the neighborhood, to be on the safe side. Streetlights at each corner cast shadows in the blowing snow. By now the news must have spread about his breaking in. The neighbors would be watching for any suspicious activity, real or imagined. Down the street neighbors were busy shoveling snow out of their drives and off the sidewalk. They were too intent to notice him. With his nearly frozen forefinger, he pushed the doorbell, his heart rate speeding up. He'd been out of his mind to come back here.

Steps sounded, moving toward the door. The porch light went on. Nora peered out the narrow window across the top of the door. Only the top of her head and her eyes were showing. *She must be standing on tiptoe,* he guessed, knowing how short she was. The moment seemed frozen in time. Her eyes below her crinkled forehead met his, and widened in bewilderment.

"It's me. Let me in," he demanded in hushed tones.

On the other side of the door, Nora fought fear and at the same time an incredible desire to see and touch Terry. He had murdered a man. Why had he come here? What might his intentions be concerning her? Her heart jumped out of rhythm, thinking fear versus love. She had loved him as a boy, and she loved him even now, no matter what he had done, no matter that he had made a mess of her house. She was weary from the effort of getting things back where they belonged.

He looked pathetic, his eyes tired and fearful, peering at her. In her eyes, the beard and mustache and the lines sketched on his face made him look older than he was. But she would always recognize him. The etching of time was no disguise. She unlatched the door, and hearing the metal scraping sound of the lock, he turned the knob and walked in. She opened her arms, and he, faltering for only a moment, stepped into her warm embrace. Her body was soft and spongy like a cushion, stamped on his memory. He would have recognized her anywhere. Except for the lines creasing her face and the flabby chin, she looked the same. She was wearing an apron like always. Without the apron she wouldn't look natural.

She basked in this rediscovered affection. All the years of despair over his fate and the loss of his presence in her life vanished like they had never existed.

Suddenly he pulled away. "Why didn't you write?" he demanded, his face contorted with anger.

"I sent several letters, but you never answered."

"I never got any letters!" He didn't believe her for a minute.

"Will took them to the post office for me," she defended herself. Instantly she knew. A revelation of truth dawned. Will hadn't mailed the letters.

"That old bugger, Will. He never sent them!" Terry exclaimed angrily.

"I am sorry," Nora wept, tears tracing the lines in her cheeks. "Will wasn't a forgiving person."

Terry felt like a knife was twisting in his gut. It would have meant the world to get a letter from her. He'd gone around like a mad lost dog, thinking that she didn't care a thing about him. Yes, letters would have made a difference. He'd had murderous thoughts about her, this old woman who had been the epitome of kindness. Memories of how she'd cooked his favorite dishes and baked pies and peanut butter cookies because he liked them shamed him now. He remembered how she'd never complained about how greasy and grimy he got working on Will's car when it broke down or when he'd changed a tire or even washed it. She'd been as kind as Will had been knuckle-headed. In his mind that old man had been as hardheaded and as hard-hearted as any criminal in prison. It was a good thing he was already dead.

Terry sat down in a familiar chair that once had boasted brightly colored peonies. The fabric was faded now and crumpled like real flowers in the fall. He looked dazed, as if he were emerging from a trance. He was weak with remorse. He could never make up to Nora for all the pain he'd caused her. His head dropped into his hands. "I am so sorry, Nora. I've really disappointed you."

"I know you are, Terry." Her voice was soothing. His heart was wrenched. He'd told himself that he had no heart. He could commit any crime and not regret it. It wasn't true.

She took a chair near him and waited. Now wasn't the time to begin lecturing or asking him what he planned to do next. If he kept on running, he'd end up dead. If he gave himself up, he'd end up in prison for the rest of his life, but it was better than the alternative.

"I'm sorry I messed up your house. Can I help put anything back?" he asked, looking around. Everything looked neat and in order. "I've made a mess of my life. I'm a mess. What can I do?"

"I'm sure you know the answer," she ventured, moved to tears by his remorse.

"And what's that?" He looked up, his voice hard, one that she hadn't heard before, one that had developed out of thirty years of being amongst other bad boys, veiled in bodies of grown men.

She reached back into her memory to recall something that might speak to him. "Do you remember how you went to Sunday school and church?"

"Of course! I remember all that stuff." His voice wasn't gruff now. His memory painted pictures of his life as it had once been.

"You liked to go. You told me when you were ten years old that you believed in God."

"And in Jesus," he scoffed.

The Love of Cars

"Yes, you did. What happened to that belief? I should have seen what was going on in your life." Nora picked up a corner of her apron and wiped her eyes.

"I suppose it fell on rocky soil." He recalled the parable. His voice held contempt. He clung to his last vestige of pride.

"It can still be transplanted into good soil." Her throat was dry, so she didn't sound like herself. Her words were barely audible, but they rang sincere in his ears.

"Do you really believe that?" He looked pitiful—so riddled with guilt—that it tore her up.

"Yes I do, Terry."

The love in her voice undid him. Wrenching sobs shook his body. He covered his face with hands that looked as soiled as his soul had to be.

"You remember how it is, Son. If you ask God for forgiveness, you can begin a new life with Him. He doesn't turn anybody away, no matter what their sin."

For her to call him "Son" after all he'd done! "Old—" he began. "I mean...Damon's wife said she forgave me."

"I'm sure she does. What's more important than her forgiveness is God's forgiveness. Can you accept that, Son?"

"I want to, Nora."

She believed him. "Pray, Son. Tell God you're sorry and that you want Jesus to come into your heart."

"'Jesus loves me this I know. For the Bible tells me so. If I love him when I die, he will take me home on high.'" Terry sang the child's hymn as a prayer. "I do believe, and I want Him to forgive me."

"Praise the Lord!" Nora raised her hands in thanksgiving.

Chapter Twenty Two

LOST AND FOUND

"My car was a rust bucket, but it got me where I needed to go," Mary wailed. "I don't have money to buy another one."

Seeing Mary in a negative mood was like trying to imagine angels without wings. The five of them were gathered around the fireplace, whose only glow now was from dying embers.

"You're safe. The twins are safe. That's all that matters. We're thankful for that!" Tom exclaimed. "Your insurance will cover theft. You do have insurance, don't you?"

"Just what's necessary in case I bashed somebody or smashed their property," Mary answered glumly. "I couldn't see spending money on coverage that didn't seem necessary. I mean, who would believe that anybody would want that old car? Besides me, that is." She smiled at this bit of humor.

"Yes, of course," Tom acknowledged soberly. "We'll find something for you to drive."

What he was really saying, Liz knew, was that he'd find, and probably pay for, a car for Mary.

The twins studied Tom, as if they might detect his inner workings. Was he as good as he sounded, or was it a front for the real man lurking beneath a gentleman's exterior? Their mother had run off and left them for a man who seemed like a good guy at first. Then the truth came out. He hadn't liked them and wanted no part of them in his life. He'd given their mom an ultimatum. If she wanted him, the girls couldn't be a part of the picture. What would Liz's choice be if she had to choose between a man and her kids? Or them?

Mary was still confused and angry. "Why would anybody take my car when there was a new car parked right next to it?"

"Who knows?" Liz shrugged her shoulders. "Bad things happen to good people. I try to remember that God is with us in all things." She dreaded telling the three girls that she was afraid for their safety and that it seemed wise for them to move somewhere else.

"Your car, being older, was easier to steal," Tom said, unwittingly giving Liz time to plan how to spring the news. "It could be hot wired and easily opened. But," he smothered a yawn, "now that you ladies are home, I need to be on my way."

Once she'd seen Tom to the door, where he had embraced her, Liz glided back to the family room, her face radiating her inner happiness. "We can talk now," she told them.

Three pair of eyes turned, wondering what there was to talk about. Donna broke the silence. "Is this Tom, whatever his name is, going to be around all the time?"

"He is the man who bought my husband's business. I care about him, and I hope he is around," she answered. She wanted to tell the world that she thought Tom was great and wonderful and that he cared about her. "You needn't worry," she went on, understanding the twins' skepticism when it came to men. "He is a decent person."

"That's what *you* say," Dana pouted.

"I know where you're coming from," Liz said. The glow continued to put a light in her eyes and understanding in her heart. "Tom isn't mean. Most men are decent and have morals. What's more important, Tom is a Christian."

"Oh, sure." Donna slumped in the chair, throwing a scornful look in Liz's direction.

"I have something to tell you that I want you to try to understand. I planned to wait until tomorrow to tell you this," she began. "It involves you too, Mary."

Here it comes. She's dumping us. They turned and looked at one another, knowing how the other one thought. The twins were more alike in thought than looks.

Liz leaned forward, her hands clasped on her knees. "I think we should move. I don't know if we're safe here, and I don't want any harm to come to you."

"You've got to be kidding." Dana groaned.

"I'd rather move than be dead," Donna declared.

"Where would we go?" Mary asked, going to the heart of the matter.

"I haven't figured that out yet. We need to pray about it," Liz answered, glad for Mary's support.

"We need to pray about it. Give me a break!" Donna muttered, disbelieving.

Liz puzzled over what to tell the twins before speaking. "According to the news, Thompkins was seen down by Cedarville. So maybe I'm worrying unnecessarily."

"It sounds like we're safe here for now," Mary said, suddenly aware that worry over her car was silly when their lives might be in danger.

"Grandma and Grandpa will take us to their house." Dana knew her grandparents cared. That's one thing she knew for sure.

The phone rang. Liz jumped, her nerves jerking as if they were on a short tether. She waited before answering. The three girls watched her, puzzled. "Aren't you going to answer?" one of them asked.

Liz shook her head. "The machine will get it. I'll answer when I know who's calling." The voice on the machine announced, "Hello. This is the sheriff's department calling. Mary Hartley gave us this number. We have a message for her." Liz picked up the receiver and handed it to Mary.

She and the twins listened to Mary's end of the conversation. A few seconds passed, and Mary broke into a grin. Hanging up, she shrieked, "They found my car! It's not banged up or anything. Isn't that too, too wonderful?" She laughed in relief. Liz and the twins, happy for her, whooped and laughed along with her. "It was over on the west side of town—Smith and Oak."

"I like that car. It runs. It's almost an antique," Dana said soberly.

"I like it because it's mine," Mary giggled.

"Hmmm, Oak and Smith. That's not far from Nora's," Liz remarked, her fingers splaying around her chin.

"One of those coincidences." Mary dismissed the thought. Just because the car was found in the vicinity of Nora's house didn't mean there was a connection between where Nora lived and where the police found the car.

At Nora's, Terry had made a decision to turn himself in. It was the only decent and honest thing to do. He felt good about it, about himself. He dreaded going back, being incarcerated for life. But he knew the Ten Commandments, and he'd disobeyed several of them, especially the one that commanded, "Thou shall not kill." He'd made some wrong choices in life, and now he had to face the consequences. He'd announced his decision to Nora.

If she'd been a lesser person, she might have told him to run. Instead, she supported him in his decision. "You took a human life. A woman is without her husband, and two kids are without a father. Now you must pay the price," she agreed. Tears of grief streamed down her cheeks. "This time I'll write you and visit you. You can be sure of it."

Terry wrapped his arms around her, and they cried together.

Needing to break the spell of sorrow engulfing them, Nora shoved him away, her nose wrinkled. "You need a shower, Terry. Get in there and take one." She motioned toward the tiny bathroom that opened off the kitchen.

Her command sounded like old times. He struggled against tears that threatened to spill over again. He knew Nora suffered when he suffered, and she'd experienced enough already. But, oh God, it felt good to experience freedom from the mean he-man image.

"Can I ask a favor of you, Nora?" he asked later, swallowing a mouthful of hamburger she'd hurriedly prepared. He hadn't eaten all day. When Nora asked if he was hungry, he told her he was starved. The words were hardly out of his mouth before she pulled an iron skillet out of the cupboard. She had hamburger sizzling in minutes.

"Depends," she answered in her own inimitable fashion.

"Can I stay here all night? It will give me something to remember when I go back to the joint." He hadn't pleaded with anyone for anything for years. "Please, Nora."

He'd seen his old room that morning when he broke in. Nothing had been changed. The quilt that had served as a spread was faded now. The throw rug beside the bed looked exactly the same. Only the curtains seemed unfamiliar. He guessed the old ones had become worn out, hanging in the west window. Absent was the graduation picture of himself on the bed stand that had been taken before he was caught with drugs. Not a single piece of his clothing hung in the closet. Nor did he find his book of automobiles. It was as if he hadn't existed or lived there. He supposed Will, feeling nothing but loathing for him, had seen to that. He guessed he didn't blame Will for the way he felt about him.

While he savored his sandwich—the best food he'd had in years—Nora was mulling over his request to stay overnight. All the grief she had felt years before returned. Terry had committed a terrible crime. She anguished over the fact that he had murdered Mrs. Pass's husband, just as she had mourned his being sentenced to prison years before. Still, her heart could not deny him. Nothing he had done could destroy the love in her heart. If it would give him a measure of comfort through his internment, who was she to deny it?

"Yes, you can stay. I'll make up the bed," she said, patting his shoulder.

While she pulled the fitted bottom sheet into place, she had second thoughts. *Will I be charged as an accomplice, for aiding and abetting a criminal?* She pushed it out of her mind. The risk was worth taking. She'd have her boy back for the night. As she pulled a pillowcase on a pillow, she couldn't see any reason why she'd be in trouble. Surely, they'd overlook her letting him spend the night when Terry turned himself in, as he said he intended to do. She had to trust him, and in God, that his restored faith would keep him honest.

As she busied herself, she wondered if Liz would understand how she could love this man. He had been like a son to her. Terry had told her that Mrs. Pass said she forgave him. Surely, then, she wouldn't hold it against her. Missy, if she knew her at all, would be happy about Terry's change of heart. Maybe she could put herself in her place. She had a son and a daughter. She'd know what it was to love regardless of what they did. She just knew it!

At eleven Nora was physically and emotionally exhausted. So was Terry. He sank down in his old bed and wept like a baby. What a fool to have completely messed up his life! He'd had a second chance when he got out of prison. He'd blown it big time.

I am still free. I could run. The thought of turning himself in and being handled like a piece of dirty laundry by the police wasn't something he wanted to think about. He could take off in the morning and maybe make it down south, maybe Mexico. It would be a long shot. *Why am I toying with such an idea? I've turned my life over to Christ. I can't turn my back on Him, not after what He did for me.* He was nothing but a foul-smelling rag, but God had changed his heart. It would be tough, but he'd grit his teeth and bear it because he was a Christian now. For Nora's sake he'd do what was honest and right.

He regretted having murdered Damon, too. The memory was like a knife twisting in his heart. Damon had been a friend, but such a sucker for going along with him. Damon had been wise not to implicate himself. Who wanted to align themselves with anybody foolish enough to stab somebody? Fortunately, the agent had lived, or he might have ended up with a life sentence. Now, for sure, he'd get life. His only consolation was that He had Jesus in his heart.

He tossed and turned, wide awake as soon as he hit the bed. Around midnight he heard Nora snoring. What a lovely sound.

He'd remember it for years. Funny, he'd detested the racket his cell mates made, sawing off logs as they called it.

It had been years since he'd uttered any kind of prayer. Now he lifted his thanksgiving to God. "Thank you for Nora, God. Knowing her, I guess I know a little better what your love is like. I'm tempted to run, but I know I can't run from you. So help me when I have to face the cops. And help me when I return to prison."

He'd planned to stay awake and savor every moment of being at home for the night, but his body fought him, exhausted from wandering around like a lost dog, stealing, going hungry, and trying to stay alive and out of the hands of the police. What a fool he'd been to murder Damon! He drifted off to sleep for a few hours, at peace with the world and with himself.

Chapter Twenty Three

Good News

Liz thought she'd have trouble sleeping after the traumatic events of the day, but—as her father used to say—she'd slept like a log. When the phone rang, jarring her out of a sound sleep, she stuck an arm out from beneath the covers and fumbled around, nearly knocking the phone off the nightstand. Raising her head enough to read the time on the clock resting beside the phone, she wondered who had the nerve to call at seven on Sunday morning. She considered letting it ring. The answering machine would record the message after four rings. But it might disturb Mary, who had a phone in her room. Who knew but it might be Mary's husband calling from Parris Island? Or Jessie? Or David? Or the sheriff, with news about Thompkins? What a relief it would be if they'd picked him up. If it were Terry Thompkins, she'd—she'd what? Hang up? If they didn't pick him up soon, she'd become a basket case. She supposed she needed to spend more time praying for the sheriff, herself, Thompkins, and Nora, of course.

"Hello." Her mouth was dry, but she managed not to croak like somebody awakened from a sound sleep and as if she weren't in total control. If it were Thompkins, she'd definitely hang up. She had nothing to say to the man.

"Missy, it's me, Nora."

What a relief. Liz scooted back under the warm covers. Brassy rose, jumped across her feet, and flopped down on her ankles. "Is something wrong?" She hoped Nora would make it short so she could rest a while longer, even go back to sleep until eight. What was so urgent that Nora couldn't wait until a decent hour to call? Was she calling to say she was too upset to clean that week? Or sick? Thanksgiving was only four days away.

"Yes, and no, Missy." Nora cleared her throat, hacking morning mucus, a by-product of year-round allergies, not the most pleasant sound in her ear so early in the morning.

"Aren't you feeling well?" Liz pressed. *Something must be wrong.*

"Don't worry, Missy. I'm okay. I'm so happy—and unhappy too." She sniffed and paused to blow her nose. If Liz wasn't mistaken, Nora was crying. She felt guilty for thinking selfish thoughts.

"I wanted to tell you before you heard it on the news," Nora began.

"I don't usually watch television on Sunday mornings. What's worth listening to this morning?" She immediately regretted being flippant. Had somebody reported seeing Terry? Was he in the area? Had he killed somebody else? But Nora said she was happy and unhappy.

"Terry stayed here all night." Nora reported this as calmly as if she were talking about the weather.

"What?" Liz bolted upright. "You must have been scared out of your wits. How horrible for you!"

"Oh, it wasn't horrible at all. It was wonderful, Missy. My boy was here with me."

"Nora! You can't mean that."

"Oh yes, Missy, I do!" Nora declared emphatically. "He came to the door, and I couldn't turn him away. We talked. He was so miserable. Then you know what? He accepted Jesus into his heart."

"Hmmm." Liz was skeptical. More often than once she'd heard reports about a criminal professing to believe in order to get a lesser sentence. Only yesterday that man, that murderer, had heckled her on the phone, terrifying her. There was no way Nora's claim could be true.

"It's true, Missy, Terry is a changed man. God worked a miracle in his heart."

"You're sure? Where is he now? Is he still there?" The questions slipped off her tongue like liquid gold. She was highly skeptical of Terry's supposed confession. Alarm bells went off in her head. For Nora's safety, she needed to hang up and call the police.

"He's gone." Nora was crying now, remembering how the police cars screeched to a halt in front of her house, sirens going, not more than five minutes after Terry called. The scene that followed would be forever etched in her memory. The police jumped out of their cars, guns drawn, even though she'd gone out and stood on the porch and told them that Terry was giving himself up, as he said he would. Neighbors had come out of their houses in their nightclothes, gawking. The memory of how Terry had been manacled and shoved into the police car was almost more than she could bear.

"You're safe now."

"Poor Terry. He'll be going back to prison. For life." Nora ignored Liz's concern for her safety. She felt as if someone had their hands around her throat so that she had trouble speaking.

"The police tracked him to your house? That's good." Liz felt brain dead after sleeping so soundly. Naturally Nora was relieved that Terry was in police custody. She was relieved for herself and for the girls, her family, and everybody concerned.

"No. Terry called the police and turned himself in. The police came after he called."

Slowly she began to comprehend what Nora was telling her. Terry Thompkins had turned himself in after making a profession to faith. He was a modern day Paul, a murderer who met God and was a changed man. It was incredible. But what comfort could she offer Nora? Should she say she was sorry? Or glad? She asked for more details of Terry's supposed conversion.

Nora answered her questions with the clairvoyance of a mind reader. "Now do you understand, Missy, why I'm happy and sad too? But mostly happy? My Terry is a Christian. That's the best part. The terrible part..." Nora searched for words. "The terrible part is he'll be spending the rest of his life in prison, thinking about how he killed his friend. I am glad Michigan doesn't have the death penalty."

"I understand, Nora. It's wonderful that Terry is a Christian. What a miracle! I know it's an answer to your prayers. It's a blessing after all the heartache you've suffered."

"If only he hadn't murdered your husband!" Nora wailed. "I understand if you don't want to see me again."

"Nora, like I told you before, what Terry did was *his* crime, not yours. I want you to continue working for me." Selfish reasons swam into her head like trash floating in clean water. She needed Nora's help getting the house ready for Thanksgiving. "I value your help, Nora. You will help me this week?"

"I'm not sure, Missy. If there's anything I can do to help Terry, it will take—what they call first priority. I can do anything to help Terry, even if it's seeing him before they take him back to prison. I'm not sure what happens next."

"Of course, Nora, I understand. Don't worry about it. I'll make out somehow."

Liz hung up, exuberant with relief. She was rid of the burden of fear and endless anxiety. Her nerves had been stretched to the breaking point. "Thank you, Lord God," she said, lifting her hands over her head in praise. "And forgive me for not trusting in your care and love."

Racing upstairs to Mary's room, she barged in without knocking. "Mary, we're safe! We don't need to worry any more about Terry Thompkins. He's a Christian. He turned himself in. Isn't this too wonderful? I'm going down and tell the twins. I'm going to call Tom!"

"And David and Jessie," Mary reminded her, sitting up and rubbing her eyes.

"And Cory. And the pastor! I suppose I can wait to tell them at church." Sinking down on Mary's bed, she chattered on. "Terry Thompkins is free. You know what I mean. He is free in spirit. What a wonderful Thanksgiving blessing for Nora." She paused and then rushed on. "Now all I need to think about is getting ready for Thanksgiving. I can hardly wait until the kids come home."

"Will Nora be coming to help?"

"Nora says she might be busy holding Terry's hand," she said scornfully.

Mary peered at her with a surprised expression. She'd rarely heard Liz say a mean thing about anybody. On the other hand, she excused her. Liz was an imperfect human being saved by grace like every believer.

"I'm sorry. I shouldn't have said that," Liz apologized, waving her hands as if she could erase the remark. "I haven't said my prayers today. My human self jumped out."

"Knowing you're not perfect gives me hope," Mary quipped. Locking her hands behind her head, she said she'd help with Thanksgiving. "Except for cooking." She giggled.

"I haven't had a chance to tell David and Jessie about the twins living here." *And should I invite Tom to dinner?* Her mind drifted to personal concerns. Most likely he would eat dinner with Maggie. She could invite him for coffee and dessert later in the afternoon. It seemed to her that the kids would like to meet the man who bought the plant. Or was that wishful thinking? To be perfectly honest, she hoped they'd like him whenever they met him.

"I'm relieved to hear the news about Nora's son, but now I'd like to sleep a while longer," Mary said, stifling a yawn.

"Sure," Liz said absently. "Sure," she repeated, thinking to herself that, yes, she'd invite Tom. She'd introduce him as a friend. Being young and familiar with the modern-day acceptance of male and female relationships, they certainly should be open to giving her that freedom.

Chapter Twenty Four

THANKSGIVING REVELATIONS

David, Jessie, and David's girlfriend, Janice, drove in at one o'clock on Thanksgiving Day afternoon. They had classes until late Wednesday and didn't start home until early Thursday morning. The ten-hour drive had been tense, with hazardous driving conditions and heavy traffic. Regardless of how exhausted they were, they bounced into the house with the buoyant energy typical of youth. Liz had prayed for their safe arrival, but she worried nevertheless. She was always taking things back from the Lord that she'd placed in His hands.

As they walked into the house, Janice's jaw dropped. "David, this is beautiful!" Her reaction wasn't put on, Liz could tell.

David chuckled, "You didn't know I'm a rich boy."

"Thank you," Liz said, giving David and Jessie a hug, and then Janice. *This girl is delightful.* With two-and-a-half days before they left, there was time to get to know her. By then she'd know if this girl was the real thing, the one for David. *You're not to judge, and you're not David.* She couldn't help herself. God had given her wisdom to discern the intent and hearts of others. She wanted David to marry a girl who would be a true helpmate.

She approved of Janice's appearance. Her jeans weren't so tight that they threatened to split any second, nor was her navel on display, which in Liz's eyes was a big plus. Her blond hair was thick, lustrous, and shoulder length. It fell in her face, and she constantly pushed it back, but Liz allowed her that one imperfection. Liz's critical eye detected that she wore makeup, skillfully applied. It added rather than detracted from her good looks. *So you're rating her on her appearance. But appearance spoke almost as loud as words. It reflected on what lay inside people—their attitudes and their respect for others.*

"I have hot chocolate or soda—whichever you prefer—after you freshen up," she called after them. They were trooping up the stairway with their bags. "And Jessie, I neglected to tell you. Janice will be staying in your room. I hope you don't mind, Janice?" There were twin beds in Jessie's room. She'd insisted on them in the event that a girlfriend stayed overnight.

Janice looked down at Jessie, who stood on the step below.

A puzzled expression squeezed Jessie's finely plucked eyebrows together. "We have two extra bedrooms," she objected. Her face screwed into a pout, totally ignoring how Janice might be affected by her words.

"Mary has one, you know. And I sent the drapes back that were up in the spare room. They were faded already. Murray's is going to replace them."

"You should furnish the basement bedroom," Jessie snapped.

"I have, but there are two girls staying with me. That's their bedroom."

"I don't mind if there aren't drapes," Janice said, a worried look on her face. The last thing she wanted to do was cause confusion in David's family.

"I still don't get it. What is going on with all these strangers living here?"

How did I fail as a mother that Jessie is so selfish? And rude. Jessie needs to grow up, think of someone else besides herself. But now I know Janice is a peace-maker.

"I'll explain what's going on once you get settled and come down to dinner." She fixed her attention on Jessie, who gave her a querulous look. Her mother's voice and demeanor were unfamiliar somehow. What it was, she couldn't put her finger on. Her mother had never been unfair before. So unreasonable. Surprised by her mother's refusing to give her her way, she searched Liz's face for some clue and found none. Mom did look prettier somehow. She wore her hair in the same, familiar old style; her makeup was flawless as always; she didn't appear to have lost any weight. But there was a light in her eyes she didn't remember. At a loss to discern the change in her mother, Jessie turned and stamped upstairs, her chin held high, her shoulders straight as if she were fearful the chip on her shoulder might fall off.

At the same moment David, viewing his mother, was struck by a vibrancy he hadn't seen before. He was surprised that the tiff with Jessie hadn't shaken her as it always had. He was glad beyond words to see her looking so happy. He'd make time to talk with her privately and see what was going on with her.

The twins appeared shortly before dinner, walking as if on eggshells. Liz had explained earlier to David who they were and how they happened to be there. He'd raced downstairs to talk with his mother while she stirred hot chocolate and made last-minute preparations for dinner.

"A regular open house," he said, surprised yet skeptical. Getting involved with these young girls would mean putting herself on the line, being available, getting involved in their personal problems. Did she fully comprehend what she was getting in to?

"It's my commitment," Liz told him, hoping for but not needing his approval. When Damon was alive, she'd been sheltered and in a sense, controlled. Any choices she made had to be a joint decision. As it should be in a marriage, she knew. In the matter of attending church, he'd ignored discussing it as long as dinner was on the table when he walked in the door. Now she was on her own, but she found herself falling into the old pattern, needing to convince David that the commitment she'd made was beneficial to her as well as to Mary, Dana, and Donna. It had brought peace and a sense of fulfillment. She had a purpose for living that went beyond herself.

"My life was centered around you kids and your father when he was alive," she began. "I loved being a mother and taking care of you and Jessie. But I always felt something was lacking in my life as you kids grew up and became less dependent on me. After you kids were gone and your father died, it seemed such a waste to have this large house and not put it to good use." She paused, hoping he understood. "The pastor preached on having purpose in your life. I decided to take in women and girls who need a place to live temporarily. I've done this in gratitude for all God has done for me. I feel fulfilled and good about myself for the first time in my adult life." Tears glistened in her eyes and a wide smile spread across her face as she finished her little speech.

"That's something else, Mom!" David marveled at how she was fairly bubbling over with enthusiasm. He'd never seen her so animated. Jumping up, he threw his strong arms around her, lifted her off the floor and hugged her. "Go for it, Mom."

Donna and Dana walked demurely into the family room, but with an attitude of "don't mess with us." They were outsiders looking in, and they were on the defensive, feeling overwhelmed by strangers. How would they be treated by Liz's kids? Ignored, looked down on? Well, who cared? They had each other.

David jumped up from his seat beside Janice and turned on his best smile. He took their hands in his and gave them a quick handshake. "Welcome."

They pulled back, recoiling like springs popping up in an old easy chair, their fists clenched, ready to slug him.

"I'm sorry. I didn't mean to offend you," he said, mortified.

"Donna and Dana," Janice interceded, "sometimes David acts before he thinks. He hasn't a mean bone in his body. He loves Jesus and everybody in the world. He gave me a hug the night we met. I thought he was too weird. I stuck around out of curiosity, so I could see if he was for real. I had to figure out what he was all about, or if he was just putting on a show."

The twins didn't buy all this talk about Jesus. It was all new, weird stuff to them. They'd wait and see if these people were for real, if they walked the walk and talked the talk, as the pastor at Mrs. Pass's church had preached about the Sunday before.

Mary fit in like an old member of the family, except with Jessie, who resented her and the twins for usurping her rights in her own home. *This would never have happened if Daddy were alive,* Jessie told herself. Her mother had gone off the deep end. Before they knew it, she'd be putting a sign out on the road, welcoming anybody that happened by.

Once they sat down to eat, the atmosphere was pleasant. They gorged themselves on the delicious food Liz had prepared. David announced that he planned to take Janice to meet some old friends later that afternoon.

"I've invited Cory and Ben for coffee and dessert," Liz said, disappointed. "You kids are like family to them. Their kids are at their in-laws this year. And I invited Mr. Kelley, the man who bought Daddy's business. I thought you'd like to meet him. They are coming about five. Could you stick around and meet them?"

"We can say 'hello.' And have dessert. I wouldn't miss that for anything," David assured her.

"The dessert, or seeing the people?" Liz joked, half serious. "I don't want to infringe on your time. I've planned nothing else while you're home."

"You invited Mr. Kelley? Why would we want to meet *him*?" Jessie was quick to pick up on Tom's name.

"He's been kind and came to our rescue a time or two," Liz offered.

"He helped me when my grandmother passed away. He helped your mom when she bought furniture." Mary spoke up, defending Liz. *Wait until David and Jessie get a load of Mr. Kelley and their mom together. Jessie will have a real tizzy then. Poor child.*

"We'll stay and have dessert," David repeated. "I'm interested in hearing about the Thompkins guy. You say he turned himself in?"

"He gave his heart to the Lord at Nora's. He's a Christian."

"You're serious? That's a modern day miracle!" David exclaimed enthusiastically. He scooped up a last forkful of twice-baked potatoes, one of his favorites.

"I'll bet. I suppose he's claiming to be a changed person." Jessie spat scornfully. "He expects to be treated as special is my guess." Turning on David, she snapped, "I don't get you, David. He murdered our father." She covered her face with her napkin to hide tears that lay just below the surface since Damon's death.

"We need to forgive him, Jessie. As God forgives us."

"Don't preach to me, David." Jessie took her napkin and slapped it on the table.

The twins were all ears. A need of forgiveness was foreign in their experience. If someone did something mean to you, you gave them back double. The thought of forgiving their father was ridiculous. But like Jessie said, how could David forgive a man who murdered his father? He couldn't have been too bad. Look at this house they lived in.

"All sin is equal in God's sight," David pressed on.

"Maybe for you, but not for me."

"I've forgiven him," Liz interjected quietly.

"I don't believe this!" Jessie pushed her chair back and jumped up. "I'm leaving. I'm going over to Amy's."

"She's home?" Liz asked, telling herself to keep her cool. Jessie's hostility pained her. When Jessie responded with a jerk of her head, Liz commandeered all the composure with which the Lord had graced her. "Have a good time," she called as cheerfully as she could manage. "See you later."

That was salt in the wound for Jessie. "I will!" she said, stamping off, muttering under her breath, but loud enough for all of them to hear, "Home will never be the same without Daddy."

After her exit, David took Janice's hand in his. "I'm sorry your first visit with the family turned out to be—what can I say? A bad scene."

"Jessie is upset over your father. He hasn't been gone that long."

"See why I love her, Mom?" David asked, jubilation in his voice. He turned and pecked Janice's cheek with a light kiss.

Liz smiled and nodded her agreement. "I'm sorry that your first impression of our family isn't the greatest. But I do appreciate your understanding of Jessie. She loved her Dad. There was no one like him in her eyes. She was the apple of his eye."

David turned thoughtful. "I'd like to meet this Thompkins and hear his testimony first hand. I'd like to know why he was so angry with Dad that he resorted to murder."

Liz debated. She folded her napkin and moved her tumbler around in a circle, weighing her words before she spoke. "Nora's the only one who could give you the details of how Terry Thompkins came to accept the Lord. She and I talked about it when she came to help me on Tuesday. Poor thing! Such a tragedy for her, the way he destroyed his second chance in life. Terry's was a simple conversion experience. The Spirit was there, and Nora took him down the Roman Road. You know, she knew the salvation scriptures. It was a joyful time for her. It cleansed the hatred from his heart, and he was a new person, just as Scripture promises."

"He is like a modern day Paul." David spoke adamantly. "But I wonder why he hated Dad. There must have been a darned good reason."

"There's no excuse for what he did. No legitimate reason under the sun. He was like so many people who are bound by hatred." Pausing and looking around the table, Liz's gaze stopped when it came to Mary. Mary and the twins didn't need to hear the rest of the story.

As if reading her thoughts, Mary slid her chair back from the table and said to the twins, "Let's go out to the kitchen. We can wash the pots and pans for Liz. The rest will go in the dishwasher."

The twins gave her sour looks, but Mary ignored them. "Dana, bring the bowl of potatoes; Donna, bring the rolls. They need to be wrapped and put away." Lifting the platter of left over turkey, she said, "Excuse us," and left for the kitchen, giving the twins no alternative but to follow.

Liz thanked her and turned to David. She looked anxiously into his face. "I hadn't planned to tell you what I know about your dad's past."

Janice began shoving her chair back. "I'll go out and help the girls."

"You stay right here," David insisted. "I don't want any secrets between us." Gripping her arm, he turned to Liz. "I want to hear whatever it is, Mom."

Liz knew from David's remark to Janice that their relationship had escalated, but that was another subject. If David felt comfortable with Janice there, it was his choice. "Your dad made some serious mistakes when he was young," she began. "And it won't be pleasant for you to hear."

"He was my father and a human. I know he wasn't perfect."

"I hope you won't think less of your father. He loved you." She impressed this on David before beginning the sad story of Damon's involvement with drugs.

"Your dad and the man who murdered him were friends in high school," she went on. "They were selling drugs, and Terry got caught."

"Dad was selling drugs! Are you sure?"

"Yes," she answered quietly. "Terry got caught. Damon didn't. Terry stabbed the officer who arrested him. He hated your father because he didn't get caught, I suppose. Your father would have served time for peddling drugs." Her throat was dry. She sipped some water.

"Good came out of it. Your father learned that you don't go along with the crowd, or in this instance, with a friend. Apparently Terry was the kind who could get people to follow his lead. Your dad followed. But he learned from experience. He was his own person from then on. He became a leader, not a follower. He was never dishonest, as far as I know, after I knew him."

David was quiet, absorbing these shocking facts about his father. When he finally spoke, his thoughts were of Jessie. "Jessie doesn't need to know this. To her, Dad was the salt of the earth. She'd hate us for telling her."

"She was special in his eyes, I know," Liz said. "She might resent us for telling her. No, I think you're right. We shouldn't tell her. Perhaps in the future, if it would benefit her in some unforeseen way."

"I am glad you told me. It softens my memory of him. I see why he was driven to maintain control of everything and everybody. He was determined to keep us heading in what he believed to be the right direction. I suppose that figures into why he didn't want me to go into the ministry. To him faith was an indication of weakness. My going into the ministry personified for him his own past weakness. Poor Dad, he didn't get it."

"I think you've got it figured right. I'm so glad that your dad's image isn't more tarnished in your eyes." She used her napkin to catch the tears of relief she felt, thankful that David had the ability to put things in perspective

David's features suddenly contorted and he cried, "I wish I had been kinder with Dad. If only I'd been more patient."

"I failed as a witness too. He obviously didn't see anything in me that made faith appealing to him. I should have been more vocal. I held my belief to myself. I was so unsure of my faith that I feared being scoffed at."

"He could do that," David remembered and nodded in agreement.

"Since I started attending Bible study and being so terror-stricken, wondering if our lives were in danger, my faith has come alive."

Janice voiced her opinion. "I'm sure Mr. Pass saw a witness here. The very fact that David chose to serve God, rather than stay and take the easy way out as the boss's son, must have made some impression."

"I don't recall if I told you that he was willing to have the nurse in intensive care pray for him. I hope that was an indication that he had a change of heart," Liz said, wistfully.

"Someday we'll know," David assured her. "Now we'll help you clean up so we'll be ready for Cory and Ben. And Mr. Kelley. *I don't understand Mom inviting Kelley. Thanksgiving is a family time, and for friends like Cory and Ben. Why is it so important that I meet him? It will be interesting to see what kind of man bought the plant.*

Chapter Twenty Five

MOM AND THAT MAN KELLEY

Liz was scurrying around cutting pies and arranging cookies on a Lenox holiday tray when the twins' grandmother called. "I'm the twins' Grandma Hardy," she introduced herself, a tremor in her voice. "My husband and I would like to visit the girls. We get so lonesome to see them. Could we come and visit? We won't stay long," she promised, a plea in her voice.

Liz had thought it was odd that they hadn't been in touch. How could she object? "Yes, of course. I'm sure they will be happy to see you."

Liz wondered what kind of people the grandparents were. The twins had been with her long enough that she dreaded the thought of their leaving. Praying for them had become a constant petition. She was rewarded when she saw indications that they were shedding their crusty shells of hurt and anger at the world. They treated her with more respect and seemed more open to her motherly guidance. To encourage bathing daily and washing their hair, Liz had supplied them with body washes, shampoos, lotions, and creams. She made it a point to comment on the way their hair shone "like those on television ads." She'd gone the extra mile by taking them to a hair salon where they had their hair cut and styled, not according to her taste, but to theirs.

"Thank you, Liz," Dana had murmured, studying herself in the salon mirror. Donna echoed her appreciation.

"Girls, it was my pleasure," Liz acknowledged sincerely.

When they'd first come into Liz's care, "please" and "thank you," were courtesies seldom used.

Above and beyond these common courtesies, she'd made a point to emphasize they were of worth as persons. God loved them and had put them on earth for a purpose. Little comments they made suggested they thought of themselves as discards. Their parents' rejection and abuse had crippled their self-confidence. Now, having contact with the grandparents, she wondered if they would reinforce what she had tried to teach the twins?

"We're having friends for dessert at five," Liz responded. "Come and join us."

"Oh, we wouldn't think of intruding. I wasn't thinking when I called. I'm so lonesome to see the girls. We saw them as often as possible when they were at Margie's."

"You won't be intruding. I'll be happy to meet you." She'd never heard the girls say anything disparaging about the grandparents. Nor had they expressed any regret that they would live with them permanently. She was curious to meet them.

The grandparents arrived shortly before the Salters and Tom. In Liz's mind they fit the grandparent image. If she guessed right, they were in their late fifties. She had to admire them for taking on the responsibility of two teenaged granddaughters. There was about them an aura of people who had experienced highs and lows in life and were survivors. Surely they were saddened by their daughter's abandonment of her children. Watching them as Dana and Donna rushed from downstairs to greet them, she saw how their faces glowed. There was no question they loved their granddaughters. Her heart sighed in relief.

"Grandma, we will miss our beautiful room here," Dana gushed.

"We'll miss Mrs. Pass, too," Donna said, amazing Liz. "Come on, Grandma and Grandpa, and see our room." Donna was pulling on her grandmother's arm.

"You'll each have a bedroom at our house." Their grandfather spoke up.

"If Mrs. Pass doesn't mind." Their grandma hesitated, looking at Liz for approval before they ventured downstairs.

"Is it okay if we take our dessert down there and sit by the fire?" Donna, ever the forward one, asked. Donna was without fear when it came to making requests.

"Of course," Liz gladly responded. She wanted private time with Cory, Ben, and Tom.

Having strangers around might hinder David from getting to talk with Tom.

The girls raced to the kitchen to get desserts and drinks. The grandparents took the opportunity to talk to Liz. "Mrs. Pass, we have a court appearance next Tuesday. If all goes as we hope it will, we'll be given guardianship soon. Our daughter gave up parental rights." The grandmother drew herself up to her full five feet, three inches, refusing to lose control of her emotions.

The grandfather stood, looking at the parquet floor, his shoulders stooped. He looked up and cast a woeful look at Liz. He was taking on a burden he hadn't planned on, but he had accepted it. "We'll give this our best shot," he assured Liz. That was enough to recommend him in her eyes.

Ben and Cory arrived soon after, and Tom pulled in behind them. Liz's heart picked up a beat as she left the Hardys to enjoy their granddaughters and rushed to open the door. Her face was flushed as she took their coats and led them to the family room. She was barely aware of the phone ringing in the background.

Tom remembered seeing Cory and Ben, and so introductions weren't necessary. He moved along with Liz as she introduced David and Janice. They rose from the hearth as Tom and Liz approached. The heat from the blazing fire had made their cheeks as rosy as Red Delicious apples.

"Tom, this is my son, David, and his friend, Janice." She was proud of her son as he stood and shook Tom's hand. She looked from one to the other, expectantly, hoping they would like each another.

"Where did Mary disappear to?" Liz asked, swirling around. She'd come to depend on Mary to be around. Just having her present was comforting.

"She got a call from her husband. She's upstairs talking to him," David said. He observed that his Mom seemed flustered like a frustrated hen in a chicken coop. All of a sudden he connected her bothered and bewildered behavior with Kelley. He wondered about his mother's relationship with this stranger. He supposed they'd seen one another out of necessity to be on a first-name basis already. But why invite him to a family gathering? Mr. Kelley appeared to be a self-confident, considerate person. Perhaps he'd been willing to be a means of support to his mother since his father's murder.

He wished there was a more pleasant word for a life being taken other than 'killed' or 'murdered' or 'assassinated.' They were ugly words, but then...the deed was ugly. The death of his father was bad enough, but to die at the hands of a murderer stirred up emotions that went beyond a normal passing. He was dealing with it. So was Mom. But it had to be much harder for her. With himself and Jessie gone, she needed a support person. Mary seemed to be just the ticket. He hated to admit it, but he'd misjudged her.

"Mary will be one happy girl," Liz said, beaming happily, interrupting David's thoughts.

"She's a peach of a girl. A hard worker," Tom added, turning to look at Liz. He was glad to have reason to shift his full attention to her. He wanted to move closer to her side, touch her arm at least.

"I thought your mom was out of her mind when she took Mary in," Cory said, directing her remark to David. Turning she smiled at Janice. "And this must be Janice?"

"Yes, this is Janice. Janice, this is my best friend, Cory, and her husband, Ben. And this is Mr. Kelley," Liz said, beaming at Tom.

"You've already introduced us, Mom," David reminded her. His mother looked prettier, somehow. Her face was flushed, too, or was she blushing? Had all the company rattled her? Was age beginning to tell on her? What was she? Forty-five? She'd married Dad a year or two out of high school. Forty-five was about right. But no, that couldn't be it. She's happy. That's what it is, he decided.

"I'm pleased to meet you. Again." Tom smiled, making light of Liz's faux pas.

"I understand you helped Mom as she went through the ordeal with Thompkins and all. Thank you for that."

"It *has* been an ordeal for her. We were kept on edge, wondering what Thompkins might do next. I worried about her, living out here in the country. Elizabeth took it in her stride. Better than lots of people would. Mary was a big help." Tom put his arm across Liz's shoulders as a brief show of admiration.

Seeing this display of affection doubled David's curiosity. Kelley didn't hide the fact that he admired his mother. The way he called her "Elizabeth" seemed significant. It was shocking, somehow, to think of his mother being special to a man. Or loved in a romantic way, if that were a fact. His mother was human and entitled to being loved and protected by a man. The idea was plenty hard to swallow. It hadn't been that long since Dad died. Somehow, he resented her disloyalty to Dad's memory. Dad had his shortcomings. From what he'd observed growing up, he lacked in the area of affection. But Dad, he would bet, had been loyal to her. He'd never seen anything to make him believe otherwise. Mom owed him respect in that sense. Furthermore, how much did Mom know about Kelley?

His thoughts were interrupted by a burst of laughter. "You never told me that story, Elizabeth," Kelley was saying.

"Yes, one of the girls in the office said there was a rumor going around that the person buying the plant was planning on turning it into a casino."

"Rumors fly faster in Middleton than a 747," Cory chuckled. "I guess it never got on the grapevine that Liz threatened to ram a woman with her grocery cart if she didn't move out of her way."

"I don't believe it!" Tom said, a grin on his face. He guessed it was true from the guilty look on Liz's face.

Pushing her chair back, Liz said, "Let's go to the dining room. It's easier to juggle cups and napkins and whatnot. Then I'll play Paul Harvey and tell you the rest of the story."

Once in the dining room, Liz placed Tom at the head of the table. She took the place beside him. Seeing Kelley sitting in Dad's place riled David even further. He was amazed at himself for feeling this sense of loyalty to his dad. *You are confused,* he mused. Determined to put aside his anger, he urged his mother to tell why she had threatened some woman in the grocery store.

"She accosted me while I was shopping for groceries and made a big scene." As she began telling the story, she was dumfounded at the anger welling up within herself. Anger at the woman and anger at Damon for not telling her his plans to sell the plant. Or that he had sold it. Except for the fact that she'd lost her temper, there was nothing really funny about the incident at all. Losing her temper wasn't funny, or anything to be proud of.

"So what was she angry about? Had you taken something she wanted and there was none left?" Ben asked. Cory hadn't told him this story.

"She was angry because the plant was sold, and she thought her husband was going to be out of a job. She accused me of being in on the decision to sell. I had nothing to do with the sale of the plant. I didn't know Damon had sold the plant until I read it in the paper."

The longer Liz talked, the more indignant she became, and she was embarrassed at her delayed reaction. Damon had locked her out of his life in many ways. It demonstrated a gross lack of respect and trust, and she hadn't deserved such treatment.

He had never confided in her about his drug dealing either, or about Terry Thompkins. If he'd told her he'd received threatening letters from Terry, she might have suggested he write to him, or that he take the letters to the police. But, no, Damon had been too proud to admit that he'd needed help or that he'd done anything wrong. The more she thought about how Damon had shut her out of much of his life, the more indignant she became.

Cory, realizing how upset Liz had become, finished the story. "The woman parked her cart in front of Liz's and wouldn't let her pass. Liz told her to move, or she'd ram her. Can you picture Liz threatening to ram anybody?" Everyone chuckled, wagging their heads in surprise, except for David. He didn't disapprove of Liz's behavior as much as what the story revealed about his mother and dad's relationship.

Liz regained her composure and put a new slant on the story. "I think about what would happen if that woman walked into church and saw me. She'd leave."

"It would be her loss." Tom spoke up, defending Liz. *If Damon were alive, I'd be tempted to bust him in the jaw. But it wouldn't have done any good. He was so blind he didn't appreciate Liz. He never acknowledged her as a helpmate.*

David, who moments ago had been upset with his mother and Kelley, had received a broader view of his parents' marriage. Mom hadn't been appreciated or recognized for having a good head on her shoulders. *Why hadn't Dad confided in her? Mom wasn't stupid. Surely she would have given a wise measure of input to any decision he made. If nothing else, she would have been a sounding board to listen as he sorted through business options.*

Mom had acted as his champion, too, when he announced he was going into the ministry. She told Dad that his choice was admirable, that she was proud of him. Dad's remark, directed at Mom, still cut him to the core. "Admirable! What do you know about it? You don't know anything about what it's like outside these four walls. Neither does he." Dad had pointed at him with a scowl that only *he* could give.

"David, your mom wants to know what you prefer to drink." Janice nudged him, breaking through his dark cloud of disturbing thoughts.

"Oh, I'll take coffee with caffeine. I need the straight stuff," he answered, attempting to keep his response light. Turning to Kelley, he asked how the business was going. Did he like it?

"I'm still getting my feet wet, as they say. By the way, I found some drawings of your dad's for a new, more modern line of furniture. I'm figuring out the cost before I implement the production. Mike Rule is a big help with the finance and accounting. I'd like to get your mother's opinion of the designs. It's good to have a woman's perspective. That is, if she wants to. And if she has time." He smiled at Liz.

"I'll be delighted!" she said, beaming at him. *Tom will make me a full partner in his life. And I do forgive Damon. In his own way, he was faithful. From knowing his parents, I suppose he picked up behavioral patterns from them.*

David heaved a sigh.

Janice, sensing his inner turmoil, grasped his hand under the table.

Liz, thinking he was tired after the hard drive, sympathized with him. "You've had a long day, David. Would you like a second cup of coffee? It will help to perk you up."

"I'm sure it will," he agreed, holding his cup while Liz refilled it. Turning his attention back to Tom, he told him he'd like to see the drawings his dad had drafted. "I knew Dad designed his own furniture, but he never wanted me around when I was a young kid. So I stayed away from then on, I guess."

"Come anytime tomorrow, or on Saturday if that fits better into your time at home," Tom told him. He welcomed the opportunity to get to know David better. Liz loved him dearly. For her sake, he wanted David's acceptance. He'd seen David watching him and Elizabeth. He'd like the boy to know his intentions regarding his mom were honest and above board.

"Tomorrow morning sometime," David said soberly.

As Tom prepared to leave later that evening, he took Elizabeth briefly into his arms. Cory and Ben were standing there, waiting to leave, when he did. "It was good spending time with David. I look forward to seeing him tomorrow. I'm sorry I didn't get to meet Jessie. Maybe another time."

"She'll be a hard nut to crack," Cory said, running at the mouth, as was her custom.

Tom had no idea what she was talking about and thought it better not to go there.

He shook Ben's hand and left.

Chapter Twenty Six

TOM AND DAVID

Tom had Damon's drawings spread out on the drawing board when David showed up the following morning. David acted congenial enough, but Tom sensed his nerves were as tight as a bowstring and that he was putting on a show of self-confidence. Besides being leery about him, the shop where his dad had spent much of his time was sure to have brought back scores of memories. As they bent over the drafting board, they found refuge in studying the designs.

"Dad had a talent for design," David said reflectively, straightening and looking at Tom.

"He certainly did. And it paid off."

"He made a good living, that's for sure. He never told us kids what his income was, but we had everything," David agreed, going on in a thoughtful vein. "The plant employed people in Middleton who wouldn't have had jobs otherwise. I guess he didn't let mom know the worth of the business. Maybe he thought he was sheltering her. I don't know."

Tom had no intention of getting into the subject of Damon's money and his relationship with Elizabeth as far as the business. He did want to clarify that the money from the sale of the business, which was now in Liz's bank account, was hers. If they married—and it was his intention that they would—then it would remain hers to use as she saw fit. He imagined she would pay for David's seminary schooling. Perhaps she'd choose to give a sum to David and Jessie as their inheritance. It would be her choice. The subject of money aside, he waited for the right moment to talk to David about his feelings for Elizabeth.

Tom continued to study the drawings, waiting for David to say what he had to say, or ask. Finally, he took pity on David. "Your father provided a beautiful home for your mother and you kids," he ventured.

"Mom deserves the best," David said, his youthful brow creasing under a wayward lock of hair. Tom thought his profile resembled Elizabeth.

"She certainly does." Tom crossed his arms and rubbed his jaw. "I'll cut to the chase. I think your mom is a terrific lady. And I think you're concerned about our relationship."

David became tongue-tied. This man was his senior, which gave him the advantage of experience and confidence. As he mulled over a response, Tom went on. "Your mom and I haven't officially dated yet. I've seen her several times—at the office and in her home. Out of respect for your dad, we've kept our relationship…ah…straight. But believe me, when a decent time of mourning has passed, I'll be on her doorstep every chance I get. I hope she'll agree to marry me."

"I do know how it is to care about a woman." David's tone was adamant.

"I'm asking your blessing. I sincerely believe God brought your mother into my life."

David saw some humor in the situation. If he'd had any reservations about Tom, they were gone now. Here was a man old enough to be his father, asking for his blessing. It was a rare situation. "I'm happy for Mom. From what I understand, you're a Christian. In my book, that's the number one priority." He reached out and shook Tom's hand.

"Jessie may be a little difficult, if that's the right word," David warned. "She adored Dad. I'm sure she'll resent Mom having another man in her life."

"We'll pray about it. I'll not let her come between Elizabeth and me." There was only the slightest hint of a smile on Tom's face as he spoke.

David knew this man wasn't fooling. He wouldn't give an inch when something mattered deeply to him. Jessie would find that out for herself sooner or later.

EPILOGUE

The following year passed slowly for Liz and Tom. They spent as much time together as they could squeeze out of a day, while they yearned for the time when they could marry.

The next summer, Tom put David to work in the factory during his time off from school. It gave him the opportunity to earn some money, even though Liz had assured him she would pay for his seminary schooling. He had retorted, "I want to earn my own way."

In the matter of whether or not to give David and Jessie their inheritance, Tom suggested she discuss it with the pastor. Liz's kids might resent him if he had anything to do with her choices. Pastor Brown advised her to wait until they were twenty-five, not because David would use the money unwisely, but because they thought Jessie wasn't mature enough. Let her graduate from college and earn some money. Then she might value an inheritance more. David would be eligible for his half.

Liz kept a third of what would have been David and Jessie's inheritance. She learned of a hospital where children of drug addicts were treated and gave her money to that charity.

David sympathized with her decision. One day she might tell Jessie the details, but not now.

Tom offered to hire Jessie, too, but she refused. Instead, she took a job at Middleton's local Laundromat for the summer and suffered the heat and humidity there. For months she wanted nothing to do with the man who turned her mother into mush the minute she set eyes on him. "I never saw you act that way with Daddy," she charged.

"We're older and know from experience how fortunate we are to have someone who appreciates and loves us," Liz replied, knowing what she said was falling on deaf ears.

Early in the fall Tom took Elizabeth to dinner and officially asked her to marry him. "If you hadn't asked me, I was going to ask you," she said, giggling and glowing with happiness. The diamond he slipped on her finger was huge.

Of course, Cory made one of her wisecracks. "Are you sure it's the real thing? Do carrots grow that large?"

"This one did," Liz countered, holding her hand so that the diamond glittered and flashed ribbons of light in the kitchen sunlight.

Nora visited and wrote Terry in prison. She took him a Bible and counseled him about reading it every day. "Stop worrying, Nora," Terry said. "We have a Bible study here in prison."

David visited Terry too. Terry expected David was suspicious about his claim of faith, which was quite true when David first visited him. David had quizzed him about his beliefs. Terry's responses assured David that he loved Christ and that he was sorry for what he had done.

"If it would change anything—you know, bring Damon back—I'd serve a dozen life sentences. Or more," he said, tears sliding down his sallow complexion. "And you gotta believe that I hate being locked up." David had to believe him.

Before Liz and Tom set a date, Liz discussed her commitment with Tom. "I need to know, will you object if I continue to open the house to women who are in need of a place to stay temporarily?"

"I don't mind at all," he said, smoothing her hair with his hand. "We'll manage to have privacy. The house is large enough. And most women enjoy seeing some romance."

Epilogue

She blushed with happiness.

"And you don't mind living in this house that Damon built?"

"I never saw him living here," he responded thoughtfully. "You're settled here, and I'm busy enough with managing the factory. Moving would be a headache. With your permission I want to do some landscaping, make the place as welcoming on the outside as on the inside."

"The house will be yours too. You don't need my permission."

"We can plan what we want to do together," he promised her.

Mary left after Brad was selected for special training as a paralegal and was stationed at Jacksonville, North Carolina. Grateful to Liz and Tom, she kept in touch and returned for their wedding, staying in the room that had been hers when she'd lived there.

So it was settled. Liz continued to open her house to any woman who needed a temporary place to stay. She broadened her commitment by doing what she loved to do—baking bread. When visitors appeared in church, she spread goodwill by delivering a loaf of freshly baked bread to welcome them. She took loaves to shut-ins and to those celebrating anniversaries and birthdays. As time passed, she grew to know the people of the church until they were like family, a family of God.

Her servant's heart expanded as she grew to know and love God more deeply and sincerely. She married Tom, whose background in the lumber business, and whose personality and ingenuity, made the plant a prominent one in the industry.

Nora found happiness in writing to and seeing Terry, but after a year she decided to sell her house and move closer to the prison in downstate Michigan.

So out of tragedy there grew new beginnings and new-found joy in life. Even Jessie decided it was futile to frown on her mother's future with Tom. She and Cory stood up with Liz in the wedding, Jessie acting as maid of honor.

Sheriff Dawson, meeting Liz in town one day, asked jokingly if she'd consider acting as a consultant in unsolved cases.

Liz didn't take the suggestion as a joke. "If I can be any help, just let me know," she responded. Unwittingly, she had set the stage for new involvement in Middleton.

To order additional copies of this title call:
1-877-421-READ (7323)
or please visit our web site at
www.pleasantwordbooks.com

If you enjoyed this quality custom published book,
drop by our web site for more books and information.

www.winepressgroup.com
"Your partner in custom publishing."

LaVergne, TN USA
28 December 2010
210395LV00001B/103/A